A Family
for the Soldier

Carolyne Aarsen

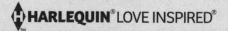

Special thanks and acknowledgment to Carolyne Aarsen for her contribution to the Lone Star Cowboy League miniseries.

Recycling programs for this product may not exist in your area.

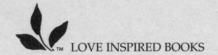 LOVE INSPIRED BOOKS

ISBN-13: 978-0-373-81882-2

A Family for the Soldier

Copyright © 2016 by Harlequin Books S.A.

www.Harlequin.com

Printed in U.S.A.

But those who hope in the Lord
will renew their strength. They will soar on wings
like eagles; they will run and not grow weary,
they will walk and not be faint.
—*Isaiah* 40:31

To my dear husband,
who knows everything and still loves me.

Chapter One

The hospital room felt suddenly too small.

Chloe clutched the chart of her patient, Ben Stillwater, as his twin brother, Grady, limped through the doorway of Ben's room. In spite of the single crutch supporting him, Grady's presence filled the space.

He stood taller than she remembered. Broader across the shoulders. His eyes had taken on a flat look, though, all emotion leeched out of them; lines of weariness bracketed his mouth. It was as if his time serving in special ops in Afghanistan had shown him sights he wanted to forget.

"Hello, Chloe," he said. His chocolate-brown eyes, shaded by dark eyebrows, drew her in as his eyes shifted to her left hand. Chloe unconsciously flexed her fingers. Though her divorce from Jeremy had been finalized a mere four months ago, Chloe had removed her ring eight months before when she'd discovered Jeremy had been cheating on her.

"A lot of things have happened since you went away from Little Horn," she said, setting Ben's chart aside, then covering his legs with a sheet. He looked so pale compared to his twin brother, who now joined her at the foot of the bed.

She had come into Ben Stillwater's hospital room hoping to do some physical therapy with him. But for the moment, all thoughts of her patient fled as the man who had once held her heart came to stand by her side.

"I know. My cousin Eva getting married, among many other things," he said.

All of Little Horn had buzzed with the news of the injured vet's return from Afghanistan two days ago, the day after the New Year had been rung in, the day of his cousin's wedding.

Eva Stillwater and Tyler Grainger had been engaged since Thanksgiving, but they had surprised everyone by announcing that they'd decided to get married as soon as her cousin Grady could come home.

"I heard it was a lovely ceremony," Chloe said. "I'm happy for them."

"Me, too. I think they wanted to start adoption procedures as soon as possible. That's why she stepped up the date." He held her gaze. "It's good to see you again."

Chloe gave him a tight smile, disturbed at how easily old emotions had intruded. She'd known she would run into him eventually. She just wished she could have had some advance notice.

So you could have put on some makeup? Do your hair?

You're a divorced woman and he's a war vet with an unexpected child, she reminded herself. *And you have other complications. Too tangled.*

Besides, she had promised herself when she discovered Jeremy's cheating that no man would hold her heart again. No man would make her feel vulnerable.

"I'm sorry. I'll leave you alone to spend time with your brother," she said, moving past Grady only to come face-to-face with her stepsister.

"Hello again, sister of mine," Vanessa Vane said, tossing her red hair, her bright smile showing off thousands of dollars' worth of dental work and a puzzling nervousness. Vanessa had never been one to show anything but overweening self-confidence.

Last month she had waltzed into Little Horn, crashing the Lone Star Cowboy League's annual Christmas party and laying claim to Cody, the baby who had been dropped off at the Stillwater ranch four months earlier. Vanessa had cried crocodile tears, telling anyone who would listen how badly she felt about abandoning Cody at that time. She should have owned up that Grady was the father and stayed around.

But she was back now and wasn't that great?

For Chloe, not so much. Vanessa's redheaded vivaciousness was a bright contrast to Chloe's wavy brown hair and calm demeanor. And whenever Vanessa saw Chloe she liked to remind her of those differences, as well as the deficiencies of Chloe's now-deceased father, Vanessa's stepfather.

"Hello, Vanessa. How's Cody doing?" Chloe asked.

Though Chloe had heard Grady and Vanessa were an item a year ago, seeing Cody, the physical evidence of their relationship, created a surprising and unwelcome heartache.

"He's great. Such a sweetie." Vanessa smiled up at Grady, batting her eyelashes.

Grady's own eyes narrowed and he didn't return her smile, which surprised Chloe. Vanessa's expression grew taut as she looked from Grady to Chloe again, and her auburn hair glistened in the lights of the hospital room. "Isn't my baby adorable?"

"He is," Chloe agreed, wishing she could be less inane. More sparkly and interesting.

Like her sister.

Every time Vanessa came into a room, eyes were

drawn to her; men took a second look at her long red hair, slim figure and vivacious personality.

"Can you give me any information about my brother, Chloe?" Grady's resonant voice broke in over Vanessa's prattling. His eyes, deep set and dark, held hers in a steady gaze, resurrecting old feelings she couldn't allow. "Do you know when he'll come out of it? Do you know if there will be any long-term damage?"

"Don't be silly, Grady," Vanessa put in, walking past him to stand beside Ben's bed. "Chloe can't tell you anything about your brother. She's only the physical therapist."

Chloe ignored Vanessa, unconsciously tucking back a strand of hair that had freed itself from her ponytail. "The only thing I can tell you is that he will experience some measure of muscle atrophy, given how long he's been in a coma." Chloe put on her professional voice, trying not to let Vanessa's patronizing attitude get to her. "The range-of-motion exercises we perform on him will help maintain as much of his muscle tone as possible and at the same time prevent sensory deprivation."

"Ooh. Long words," Vanessa said, the joking tone in her voice negated by her flinty look. "Still trying to impress Grady? I wouldn't bother."

"Do you know anything about the coma?"

Grady continued, obviously ignoring Vanessa. "At all?"

Chloe heard the hurt and fear behind his questions. She guessed the bond identical twins often shared made him more anxious.

"I only know what you know," she said. "The fall from the horse was the root cause, but there have been no other internal injuries that we can ascertain, no brain injury. No hematomas." She stopped herself there. As Vanessa had said, she wasn't a doctor. "You'll have to speak with his doctor to find out more."

"Thanks for that information at least," Grady said, his smile holding a warmth that could still make her toes curl.

"You're welcome," she said, trying to convey a more brisk and professional tone. "We hope and pray he will come out of it. That's all we can do."

"I'll take care of the hoping and leave the praying to those more capable." The bitterness in Grady's voice made Chloe wonder again about his war experiences overseas and what they had done to his once rock-solid faith.

"How long are you back for?" Chloe asked, holding up her head, determined not to let the effect he had on her show.

"For good. I got an honorable discharge from the army. I'm home."

She forced herself not to look at the crutch he leaned on to support himself.

"We can all be so thankful Grady made it back from Afghanistan. And a hero to boot," Vanessa said, the edges of her lips growing tighter, as if she had to work to maintain her vivacity.

Each word she spoke felt like a tiny lash. Her stepsister had known Chloe had a crush on Grady when they were in high school. In fact, once Vanessa had discovered this, she'd made an all-out attempt to charm and captivate Grady just to spite her. Chloe, a tomboy at heart, had known she couldn't compete with her glamorous stepsister, so she'd given up on that dream.

Given that Vanessa claimed to be the mother of Grady's supposed baby, Chloe could only reason Vanessa still held some attraction for him.

"I still can't get over how much Grady and Ben look alike." Vanessa gave Chloe an arched look as she fiddled with the sheets draped over Ben's body.

"They do look similar," Chloe murmured, trying to find an opportunity to make her escape while her stepsister chattered away.

"Similar? They are like two peas in a pod," Vanessa said, her narrowed gaze flicking from Ben to Grady. "If it weren't for Ben being flat on his back, you'd never know the difference. And did you know that twins have identical DNA?" she asked, turning to the cards on the windowsill.

And why did Vanessa think she needed to impart that particular piece of information?

"I'll leave you to visit with your brother," Chloe said, taking another step toward the door.

To her surprise and shock, Grady touched her arm, as if trying to make a connection. "It's good to see you," Grady said, lowering his voice. His eyes held hers.

Unable to look away, Chloe felt her heart quicken. Then a faint queasiness gripped her. Vanessa called out again and she dismissed the emotion as quickly as it came.

Vanessa claimed that Grady was the father of her child.

And Chloe had enough problems of her own.

Chloe's reaction to his wound still stung.

Grady fitted his crutch under his arm and made his way over the snow-covered sidewalk to the ranch house. The chill January wind biting into his face promised bitter weather to come and seemed to sum up how he felt. Vanessa had driven him in her car to the hospital. Grandma Mamie's car and Ben's truck filled the garage, which meant they had to park it outside.

All the way home he replayed that moment when he'd stepped into his brother's hospital room. He would have had to be blind not to have seen Chloe recoil from him.

Not that he blamed her. A crippled soldier and, according to Vanessa, the father of a child born out of wedlock. A child from her own stepsister.

Grady knew Cody wasn't his, and though part of him wanted to tell Chloe, he knew it was neither the time nor place; he wasn't even sure if it mattered to her. He was still frustrated at how glibly the lies had tripped off Vanessa's tongue when she had confronted him at the ranch, Cody in her arms. He had come directly here once he was discharged and the first person he'd met at the ranch house had been Vanessa.

She had unleashed a stream of innuendo and falsehoods about how she and Grady had been intimate at a party that he and Ben had attended. Initially she had said he was too drunk to remember, but Grady wasn't a drinker. Nor was he the kind of guy who slept around. At all. But the DNA test had shown Cody was a Stillwater, so Grady guessed, given his brother's wild living, Ben had fathered the child at that party.

When he'd confronted Vanessa with that information she had conceded that maybe she'd had a bit too much to drink herself and quickly claimed it must have been Ben. The trouble was, though he had made it very clear to Vanessa that he wasn't Cody's father nor was he interested in her, she still flirted with him. It annoyed him and even though he didn't encourage it, he could only guess how the situation looked to Chloe. Not exactly the hero he had hoped he would return from the war as.

Injured, with the whiff of scandal surrounding him and his family.

Precisely the thing he had left Little Horn to escape after his father's debilitating injury had sent his mother away, unable to live with a crippled man. The shame of his mother's defection and subsequent divorce had caused Grady to join the army, looking for discipline and meaning to his life. It had sent Ben on a path of hedonism and self-indulgence. Their mother's death while traveling abroad hadn't helped matters, either.

It seemed both their lives had come full circle. Now he suffered from a life-changing injury that had cut short his army career and Ben lay in the hospital after being thrown from a horse. Both living echoes of their now-deceased father.

"Slow down, soldier," Vanessa called out as she got out of her car behind him. "Let me help you."

He tried not to cringe as he kept going, tucking his chin into his jacket against the cold, trying to banish the picture of Vanessa standing beside Chloe, their differences so obvious.

Chloe with her sweet, gentle smile. Vanessa with her overly loud voice and tactless attitude.

He knew he shouldn't compare, but he couldn't help himself.

Vanessa hurried ahead of him as he struggled up the stairs to the covered veranda that wrapped around the Colonial-style house. "You know, I can never figure out which of these doors to use," she muttered as she grabbed the handle of one of the double doors. She pulled it open just as Grady came close, and the door connected with his leg.

He bit down on a cry as he stumbled, his crutch slipping out and away.

"Sorry. I didn't mean to hit you." Vanessa clutched his arm as he regained his balance, pain shooting up his leg and clouding his vision.

He rode it out, then shook off her hand, frustrated at his helplessness. "I'm okay. Please."

"I'm just trying to help you," she complained as he fitted his crutch back under his arm. "You don't need to get all huffy."

"Sorry," he said, unable to say more than that as he stumped into the entrance of the house. As Vanessa closed the door behind them, heat washed over him blended with the scent of supper baking and his frustration eased away.

He was home.

Beyond the foyer a fire crackled in the stone fireplace that was flanked by large leather couches. He wanted nothing more than to sink into their welcoming depths, close his eyes and forget everything that had happened to him the past few years. The war. The secret mission he and his team had been sent on and the hard consequences.

He just wanted to find the simple in life again.

But the sound of a baby crying upstairs broke the peace of the moment and reminded him of his obligations and how complicated his newly civilian life would be.

"Grady? Vanessa? Are you home?" his grandmother called out from somewhere in the house.

Vanessa sauntered past him to the living room, ignoring his grandmother's question.

Just as Grady shucked off his heavy winter coat, his grandmother came down the stairs toward him, carrying Cody, who was fussing and waving his chubby arms.

In spite of knowing Cody wasn't his, it wasn't hard to see the resemblance. The little boy's brown eyes and sandy hair were exact replicas of his and Ben's, and he looked identical to Grady and Ben when they were babies.

He could see how people might believe he was the father. That Chloe might believe he was bothered him more than he cared to admit.

"Is he okay?" Grady asked, hobbling over to his grandmother, the injury in his leg making itself known as he faltered.

"He's just fussy. Missing his mom, I think."

Mamie Stillwater shot a meaningful glance over her shoulder at Vanessa, who was now lounging on the couch leafing through a magazine she had bought on their way back from thc hospital.

Vancssa must have caught the tone in Mamie's voice, however, because she shot to her feet, her hands out for Cody. "Hey, sweetie," she cooed, taking him from Mamie's arms and walking back to the living room. "Did you miss your momma?"

"Can I get you something to drink? Some coffee? Hot chocolate?" his grandmother asked him, her eyes still on Vanessa who sat on the couch again.

"Coffee would be great," he said.

"I'm fine," Vanessa said to her, then turned to Grady with a coy smile and patted the couch beside her. "Come and sit down, soldier," she said.

Grady hesitated, then walked over, wavering between politeness and his own struggles with Vanessa. Though he knew Cody wasn't his child, he was clearly Ben's and therefore his nephew. However, Vanessa didn't seem very motherly.

His thoughts whirled as he struggled to find the peace that had been eluding him for the past few years. Ever since that hay bale had fallen on his father and injured his back, Grady's home life had spun out of control. His father's chronic pain had created tension, which had led to fights, which finally had sent his mother away.

Living with his father had been difficult before; it had become almost impossible after the accident. Reuben Stillwater had turned into a bitter, angry and critical man.

Grady, who had often wanted to leave the ranch and Little Horn, saw his chance when he met with a recruitment officer from the army at high school. As soon as he'd graduated, he'd joined the army looking for discipline and order. He desired adventure and an escape from Little Horn. He had joined special ops, wearing his green beret with pride.

But escape had resolved the issue only temporarily. Running special ops in Afghanistan had drained him. Had created an increasing yearning for home. When he'd been injured that horrible day, he'd known his career was over.

However, coming back to the ranch to discover a woman he neither admired nor desired was telling everyone he had fathered her child wasn't the vision he'd held in his head during the lonely nights in Kandahar, Afghanistan. He had longed for the open spaces of the ranch, the simplicity of working with cattle and horses.

As he leaned back and glanced at Cody gurgling his pleasure in Vanessa's arms, a picture of Chloe flashed in his head. She looked as pretty as ever. Prettier if that was even possible, with a simple charm he remembered from their youth.

As if someone like her would look at someone like you, he reminded himself.

"He sure knows his mommy," Vanessa said, tickling the little boy under his chin. "Don't you, darling?"

His grandmother returned with two steaming mugs of coffee. She set down one within arm's reach of Grady and settled herself on the large leather couch across from them both, her eyes on Vanessa and the baby.

"Busy happenings in the county today," Mamie said, her gaze flicking from Vanessa, still absorbed with Cody, to Grady sipping his coffee. "Yesterday Tom Horton discovered a couple of his brand-new ATVs were stolen."

"They figure the same people who've been rustling the cattle and stealing equipment are to blame?" Grady asked.

"Lucy Benson is quite sure it is. This must be so difficult for her." Grandma Mamie tut-tutted. "Byron McKay is calling for her to quit as sheriff and she's not getting any closer to the culprits."

"Byron McKay likes to throw his weight around," Grady said.

"He's a big-time rancher, isn't he?" Vanessa put in, tucking Cody against her while she opened the magazine with her free hand. "I heard he's got one of the biggest spreads in the county."

"He's wealthy enough," Mamie said. "And he

likes to let the members of the cowboy league know it."

"He's not president yet, is he?" Grady asked.

"Oh, no," Grandma protested angrily, as if the idea horrified her. "Carson Thorn still holds that position and the other members will make sure Byron doesn't ever get in charge."

"This league… That's the one that threw the fancy party I was at two weeks ago. What do they do exactly?" Vanessa asked.

"The league formed over a century ago as a service organization," Grandma Mamie said. "They provide help and resources to the ranchers in the area. There are chapters all over Texas."

"What kind of help? Like with the branding and stuff?" Vanessa seemed quite interested in the dealings of the league, which puzzled Grady.

"It started to fight cattle rustling and give support when times got hard for fellow ranchers." Mamie gave Grady a warm smile. "Grady and Ben's great-grandfather, Bo Stillwater, was one of the founding members."

"They aren't helping much for all the cattle rustling going on," Vanessa said, still turning the pages of her magazine one-handed, seemingly oblivious to her little boy, now, thankfully, sleeping in her arms. "I heard that Byron McKay got some fancy machinery stolen and another cattleman lost some animals. And that town sign thingy is still gone. Not too on the ball, are they?"

"I'm sure they're doing what they can," Grady said, cradling the cup of coffee, feeling a sudden chill. Coming home to stories of a rash of thefts of cattle and machinery and equipment was disheartening. The community of Little Horn, with the help of the Lone Star Cowboy League, had always pulled together. Though he had been back only a few days, he already sensed mistrust growing between the local ranchers.

"Funny how nothing's disappeared from this place, though," Vanessa said with a sly look. "Maybe the thieves are those kids you've got working on that, what is it, ranchers something or other?"

"Future Ranchers program," Grady said, shooting her a warning look. "And you might want to watch what you say about the girls we've got helping here. The Markham sisters' ranch has been hit, as well."

"But that Maddy Coles. I mean, she's a foster kid. She probably has all kind of weird friends."

"That's enough," Grady snapped, angry at her allegations, then frustrated at his shortness with her.

Too many things were happening at once, he thought. His brother, Ben, in the hospital, Vanessa and her ever-changing insinuations, all the upheaval the thefts had caused in the community.

Seeing Chloe hadn't helped his equilibrium, either. He'd thought hearing about her marriage would ease away the feelings he still harbored, but now she had come back to Little Horn. Single and as attractive as ever.

He felt a clutch of pain in his leg and all thoughts of Chloe vanished with it. He wasn't the man he used to be and he had nothing to offer any woman. He shot a glance at Vanessa. Especially not with someone like her entangled in his life.

"What puzzles me is all the things other people are receiving," Grandma said. "The new saddles at Ruby's, the cattle at the Derrings' and the clothes for their foster children. It's all very nice and generous, but it's puzzling."

"Well, I wouldn't mind getting some of the stuff being handed out." Vanessa tossed the magazine aside then stood in front of Grady and held out the little boy, who had woken up again and was stirring in her arms. "Can you take him? I'm tired. Didn't sleep a wink last night."

Grady hadn't slept much, either, but he said nothing. Instead, he set his coffee on a nearby table and took him from Vanessa. Cody stared up at him with bright eyes and gurgled his pleasure, and Grady felt a tug on his heart. He was such a cute little guy.

"I think you should see about getting that Eva chick back, that nanny you hired," Vanessa said. "I don't think I can take care of this little boy by myself."

Then she sauntered off before Grady could say anything more.

When she was out of earshot his grandmother got up and sat down beside Grady, letting Cody grab her finger with his. "I wish we could hire Eva again, but she's married now and I want to give her time to concentrate on her husband and married life. I wish I knew what to do."

"We will take care of him," Grady said firmly. "He's a Stillwater. Our flesh and blood. Our responsibility."

But even as he spoke the brave words, he felt a tremor of apprehension. Ben lay in a coma. He had his own injuries to contend with. His grandmother was getting on in years.

If Vanessa wasn't stepping up, what would Cody's future look like? Grady knew getting married wasn't in the picture for him, so he couldn't count on creating any kind of family for Cody.

His thoughts, unexpectedly, drifted to Chloe. Her warm smile, as generous as always. Her easy nature.

He pushed them aside as irrelevant. He would never be marriage material.

His mother hadn't been able to live with an injured man; how could he expect Chloe to?

Chapter Two

"Got a new patient for you. Is Salma here?"

Chloe looked up from the makeshift desk she had been given in one corner of the physical therapy department at the doctor standing in front of her. With his droopy moustache and thick eyebrows, Dr. Schuster looked as though he should be riding the range rather than diagnosing and treating patients. Dr. Schuster had taken advantage of this impression and adopted an aw-shucks attitude that put many of his patients at ease.

However, right now he looked anything but as he tapped the file he held against his other hand, the frown on his face giving her cause for concern.

"She's gone for lunch. Can I help you?"

"I thought she would be around."

"You look worried. Is it a difficult case?"

"I've got other things on my mind," he said.

"But this patient does bother me. He said he doesn't need therapy."

"Do you want me to talk to him?" Chloe asked, not sure she could make a difference, but sometimes another voice helped.

"You mean turn on that Miner charm?" Dr. Schuster joked. Then he shook his head. "No. I can't ask that of you."

"It's my stepsister who has all the charm," Chloe returned. Ever since yesterday when Vanessa had shown up with her arm hooked in Grady's, grinning that smug Cheshire smile, Chloe had struggled with envy and frustration. So often in the years after Vanessa's mother had married Chloe's widowed and grieving father, Chloe had wished she and Vanessa could be close. As an only child she had looked forward to having a sister.

Instead, Vanessa had been difficult and contrary, trying at every opportunity to either discredit Chloe or treat her with contempt.

"Vanessa definitely has a certain appeal." Dr. Schuster's smile deepened. "She's been the talk of the town since she descended on the party last month claiming to be Cody's mother. But I doubt she has as much staying power as you."

"Words to make a girl's heart go pitty-pat," Chloe said in a dry tone and held her hand out for the file. "Who is the reluctant patient?"

"Another Stillwater. Grady."

And now Chloe's heart did, in fact, go pitty-pat. And then some. She took the folder from Dr. Schuster and opened it, scanning the contents, trying to maintain her distance.

"This patient will need quite a bit of time spent with him." Chloe flipped through the file, shifting into professional mode. "He'll need to get started sooner, rather than later, if he wants to regain full mobility."

"He only arrived Friday, last week," Dr. Schuster said. "He came to see me yesterday on the recommendation of his surgeon in the army."

"Okay. I'll contact Mr. Stillwater. See what I can do."

"Good. Great. Make sure you let Salma know, as well. I suspect once you get Grady cooperating, as senior therapist she'll be doing most of the work."

Chloe understood this, but worried that Dr. Schuster thought she wasn't as competent as Salma. He looked as if he wanted to say more, then left, his lab coat flaring out behind him as he hurried off.

Clearly in a rush, Chloe thought, setting the file aside.

She had hoped to talk to him. Tell him about her personal situation. Guess it would have to be another time.

There were no other visitors in Ben's room

when she got there, and the only sound was the faint hissing of his oxygen, the steady beeps of the monitors. "I suppose you've heard about all the happenings in and around the county," she said to him while she got him ready for his exercises. Talking to patients while she worked was part of the therapy. "Thefts and unexpected gifts and all sorts of stuff. Kind of crazy. So far, though, nothing from your place, so that's good, I guess. And now your brother is back." Chloe's smile faded as she did a series of hip flexions and abductions, thinking of Grady.

"You know everyone says you look the same. I can see some minor differences," she continued. "Grady's eyelashes are thicker. Hope that doesn't bother you, though I can't imagine either of you could care about that. And his one eyebrow slants off to one side. I think he's a bit taller. Maybe because of his army training. Makes him stand up straighter."

A cough behind her caught her attention and she flushed, suddenly self-conscious about her chatter as Mamie Stillwater entered the room holding a sleeping Cody, a large quilted diaper bag hooked over her narrow shoulder.

"I'm sorry," Mamie said. "I didn't mean to interrupt."

"I'm just doing Ben's exercises," Chloe murmured, thankful she hadn't said anything more.

"Do you mind if Cody and I watch?"

"Not at all." Chloe felt a stirring in her soul at the sight of the little boy, so innocent, his rosy cheeks begging to be touched. Vanessa and Grady's son. The thought hurt her more than it should.

At least this child has two parents. As opposed to mine.

She tried to fight the thought down. *I'll do the best I can*, she reminded herself, thinking of the child she carried. At four and a half months, she thankfully wasn't showing yet, so she hadn't told anyone. Not even her close friend Lucy. She was too ashamed. Sooner or later, however, she would have to tell the hospital administration, and then everyone else.

Mamie dropped the diaper bag on an empty chair by the window, shifted the sleeping baby in her arms and stood on the opposite side of Ben, her free hand resting on his head while Chloe did some hamstring stretches.

"You've been doing this awhile?" Mamie asked, fingering Ben's hair away from his face.

"About two years. It took me six to get my degree."

"And you came back here…"

"I was offered this job." Part-time and only temporary, she'd been told, but she'd wanted to come back to Little Horn badly enough that she took the chance it might turn into full-time work.

"I was sorry to hear about your father," Mamie said.

"So was I." Chloe had made a visit seven months ago for her father's funeral, then returned to Fort Worth and Jeremy.

How much had changed since then, she thought.

Her father's ranch had been sold, barely paying off the debts incurred against it from his accident, and Jeremy had started divorce proceedings once he'd found out she was pregnant.

She had felt rootless and lost. Taking this job had become her way of finding her footing.

Chloe moved to work on Ben's arm when the rhythmic thump of a crutch on the floor gave her another start. Grady had arrived.

She pressed her lips together, sent up a prayer for strength and continued working.

"Good morning, Chloe," he said, his deep voice creating an unwelcome shiver of awareness. She gave him a nod, her cheeks warming as he made his way around the bed. He wavered, catching the rail of the bed to steady himself. He wasn't wearing his brace today, she noticed.

"Are you okay?" his grandmother asked.

"I'm fine." His curt voice and the clench of his jaw told Chloe he wasn't fine at all. She guessed his hip was causing him trouble, as was his knee. From what she'd read in his file, he'd been shot in the thigh, damaging many muscle groups and compromising the ligaments of his knee. "Do you want me to hold Cody?" Grady asked.

"He's okay. And Chloe said we could stay while she does therapy with Ben," Mamie said in a falsely bright voice. "It's interesting to watch her work. She's very capable."

"I understand from Dr. Schuster that you'll be coming to visit me in the physical therapy department," Chloe said, piggybacking on what Mamie was saying.

"I doubt it," Grady muttered, the tightness around his mouth another indication of the pain he dealt with. "I don't have time with everything at the ranch falling on my shoulders now. And this little guy." He glanced down at Cody, touched his chubby cheek with one finger, and Chloe's heart hitched at the warmth of his smile. This man would make a good father.

Was a good father, she corrected herself.

"Plus I've got Ben and the Future Ranchers program he started at the ranch to keep me busy," he continued. I don't have time to run around for appointments that won't make a difference."

"But if you don't take care of the low mobility in your knee and hip, you could be facing chronic pain later on," Chloe suggested.

Grady shot her a frown, as if he didn't appreciate what she had to say.

"As a physical therapist, I feel I must warn you the pain you are dealing with now will only worsen with lack of treatment." Chloe manipulated Ben's fingers, half her attention on helping the one brother while she tried to convince the other to accept what she could do for him.

"The pain isn't that bad." He dismissed her comment with a wave of his hand. "I know my dad managed through his. Your dad, as well. Just have to cowboy up."

Chloe kept her comment about that to herself. She didn't know everything about his father and care. However, she still maintained that, in the case of her own father, if he had received proper care and treatment, he would have been better able to do his work. "Being tough only gets you so far," she carried on. "Your injuries will, however, only cause you more problems with lack of immediate care."

She stopped then, sensing she was selling herself too hard. Grady looked as though he didn't believe her. Didn't or wouldn't—she wasn't sure which was uppermost.

"Are you working here full-time?" Mamie asked, stroking a strand of hair back from Ben's forehead, shifting to another topic.

"I am here as a part-time, temporary worker."

Speaking the words aloud made her even more aware of her tenuous situation.

"Where will you go after this?"

Chloe shrugged, working with Ben's fingers, stretching and manipulating, not sure she wanted to talk about her hopes and dreams to start up a dedicated physical therapy clinic in town. Finding out how little was left after settling her father's estate had put that dream out of reach.

"There are other opportunities in Denton or Fort Worth, I'm sure." Opportunities she had passed up when she'd taken this job. She wasn't a city person. Coming back to Little Horn had filled an emptiness that had grown with each day she was away.

"I see." Mamie held her eyes, nodding slowly, as if her mind was elsewhere.

"I need to work on Ben's other leg and arm," Chloe said, setting Ben's hand down beside his still body. "So I'll have to ask you to come over to this side of the bed."

Just as Chloe came around the end of the bed, Cody whimpered, opened his eyes and started to cry.

"I should get something for him to eat," Mamie said, jiggling him as she dug through the large diaper bag she had been carrying. She looked over at Chloe as Cody's cries increased. "I'm sorry to ask, but can you hold him a moment?"

"Of course."

"I can take him." Grady shifted himself so he had his hands free.

But Mamie had already set Cody in Chloe's arms.

She held the wiggling bundle of sorrow. His cries eased into hiccups. His dark brown eyes, still shining with tears, honed in on Chloe's.

A peculiar motherly feeling washed over her. This little boy, so sweet, so precious. She cuddled him close and he quieted as he lay his head against her shoulder.

"You have a way with him," Mamie said, pulling a jar of baby food out of the diaper bag. "Just like his previous nanny, my niece, Eva, did."

"He is a sweetie," Chloe murmured, rocking him to keep him quiet.

"I can take him back now," Mamie said, taking the boy from her. "I should find a place I can heat this up."

"There's a microwave at the nurses' station I'm sure you can use," Chloe said, walking to the sink in Ben's room to wash her hands again.

Mamie walked out, leaving Grady and Chloe alone. She moved to the other side of Ben's bed and started with his leg exercises.

"Does that do anything?" Grady asked. "I mean, he's not participating."

"No, but it's important we keep his abductors flexed, his hamstrings from pulling." Chloe glanced over at Grady, disconcerted to see him staring at her. She dragged her attention back to her patient. "It's a type of stimulation, as well. And if we don't do these exercises, his muscles will seize up and when he gets out of the coma, he will have a much longer recovery ahead of him."

"You said when."

Chloe glanced up from Ben, thinking of the theories of coma patients being able, on a subliminal level, to hear what was said around their bed.

"I said when and I mean when," she said, her voice firm. "He will come out of this. We just have to do what we can for him while we wait."

Grady sat down in the chair, setting his crutch aside. "I like the sound of when. I have things I need to settle with my brother. Ben and I... Well, we had words before I left."

"A fight?"

"A disagreement about his lifestyle," Grady said. "I want to make it right."

Out of the corner of her eye, Chloe saw Grady drag his hand over his face. He looked exhausted. She was sure some of it was the burdens he carried, in addition to the pain.

"Then, this is a chance for you to talk to him," Chloe said, picking up Ben's arm and stretching it gently above his head. "A chance for you to tell him what you feel. Tell him how you care for him."

"So you think he can hear me?"

"I'd like to think he can." Chloe gave him a gentle smile. "Sometimes talking aloud can be as much for yourself as for him."

Grady nodded, then looked up at her, his expression growing serious. "You think it will help?"

"Confession is good for the soul," she said.

"In that case, I'll wait until you're gone. I don't want you hearing all my deep, dark secrets."

"You have those?" And how did that semiflirty note get in her voice?

"Don't you?"

She held his gaze a split-second longer than she should have, thinking of the last time she and Jeremy had been together and the repercussions of that. The child she now carried.

She had no right to talk this way to him. No right at all.

"If you're referring to Cody's parentage, I feel I need to tell you, he's not my son. At all." His gaze locked on hers, suddenly intense.

"He's not?"

"No."

Chloe seemed surprised and yet, at the same time, pleased that he wanted her to know.

"So why is Vanessa—" she stopped herself.

She almost asked him why Vanessa was acting as if she had some claim on Grady, but it was none of her business.

Yet he seemed to think she needed to know. A tiny finger of awareness trickled down her neck. Was he trying to tell her something else?

She pushed it away as she returned to working on Ben. He was simply concerned about his reputation, that was all. Besides, it seemed that Vanessa, in spite of Grady not being Cody's father, seemed to have laid her claim on Grady.

There was no way Chloe could compete with her very attractive stepsister.

A few minutes later she had finished. Before she left, she couldn't help a glance Grady's way. But his entire attention was on his brother. So she made a notation on Ben's chart then left.

Dr. Schuster stood by the nurses' station, but he looked up when she came near.

"Chloe. Just the person I need to talk to." His grim expression made her apprehensive.

She swallowed down her nervousness. "What do you need?"

Dr. Schuster tugged at his moustache, then steered her toward a small room just off the nurses' station. "I had hoped to do this in my office, but I don't have time." Another tug on his moustache. "I'm sorry to tell you this, Chloe. But I just got the word that I have to cut back on the budget. I know I promised you a job for longer than this, but I'm afraid I have to let you go. I don't have much choice."

"Excuse me?" Chloe wasn't sure she heard him correctly. "I've lost my job?"

"The position was only temporary," he reminded her.

"For a year." She fought down her rising panic, trying to maintain a professional attitude, trying not to sound as though she was pleading. "I need this job, Dr. Schuster."

Her life had been turned upside down the past four months. She had counted on this year to catch her breath, make other plans.

"I'm sorry, Chloe. You're a hard worker and I'd love to keep you. We could certainly use a fully staffed physical therapy department. But it's not going to happen. Sorry."

"When do I leave?"

"I'll pay out your two weeks' salary, but Friday will be your last day." He patted her awkwardly on the shoulder and left.

Chloe leaned back against the wall, fighting down an unwelcome urge to cry. Silly hormones, she thought, closing her eyes and breathing slowly.

Help me, Lord, she prayed. *Help me get through this.*

The prayer had been her constant refrain the

past year. Each time she felt that she had caught her balance, life spun her around again.

She covered her face with her hands, pulled in a wavering breath, then slowly released it.

"Are you okay?"

Mamie Stillwater's concerned voice behind her made her straighten and force a smile to her face before turning around. "I'm fine," she assured the elderly woman, still holding Cody, who slept again. "I'm just fine. Just tired. How's Cody?"

"He's tired, too." Mamie gave her a careful look. "I better get back to see how Ben is. You take care of yourself, okay?" She patted her on the shoulder with one thin hand, then trudged away, her own shoulders stooped, as if carrying Cody was more than she could bear, either.

Chloe gave herself a few more moments to compose herself. But as she walked past Ben's room, she glanced sideways only to catch Grady looking directly at her. She gave him a wan smile, then carried on. She had one more patient and then she was done for the day.

And where was she supposed to go after that? How was she going to take care of her child on her own? Jeremy had disappeared after he found out she was pregnant, disavowed any interest in her or her child, and she hadn't been able to find him. Nor did she have the energy right now.

Help me, Lord, was all she managed as she made her way to the next patient's room.

"Boy, does it smell bad in here."

Grady cringed as Vanessa's shrill voice echoed down the hallway of the barn.

"You in here, Grady? I need to talk to you. I'm not coming in."

"Will you excuse me a moment?" Grady said to the three young girls standing by the doorway of one of the horse stalls. "I need to speak with Vanessa."

Maddy Coles, Lynne James and Christie Markham were part of the Future Ranchers program his brother, Ben, had initiated to help high school students get extra credit. They came to the ranch whenever they could to work with the horses and to assist with their training and care.

"Do you want me to clean out the stalls?" Maddy asked, grabbing a fork from the wall.

"That would be good. Start with Apollo. Lynne and Christy, you can go outside and get Bishop, Shiloh and Chief in. Saul said he wanted to check their hooves when he comes here. I'll be right back."

The girls nodded and Maddy, eager as ever to work, stepped into the first stall.

Grady hurried down the alleyway, the thump of his crutch on the wooden floor echoing through the cavernous horse barn. A chill wind whistled toward him as he neared the open door where Vanessa stood, her winter coat wrapped around her, her mouth turned down in a grimace of disgust.

"I don't know what's nastier, the weather out here or the stink in there." She waved her hand delicately in front of her face as if to dispel the scent.

"What can I do for you?" Grady asked.

"First off, Mamie wants you to come to the house. She's not feeling that great and Cody has been crying the past half hour."

"And you can't take care of him?"

"I told you. Hire that nanny back. I'm headed to Austin. I've got a fitting for a dress I ordered. I'll be back tomorrow."

Grady could only stare at her, the suspicions that had been hovering in the back of his mind growing stronger each moment he spent with her. "So you're leaving your son with his great-grandmother?"

Vanessa shrugged. "I don't have time for this. I have to go." She turned and hurried off, her high-heeled boots slipping in the snow that had fallen overnight.

Grady watched her go, heaving out a sigh. He shouldn't have pushed her. He blamed his lapse on the steady pain in his leg and the headaches he'd been fighting the past two days. He took a deep breath and worked his way back to Maddy and the other girls. After giving them instructions for work that would keep them busy for the next hour, he hobbled back to the house to help his grandmother.

Cody's heart-rending wails were the first thing he heard when he stepped in the house.

He shucked off his coat, banged the packed snow off the bottom of his crutch, then, moving as fast as he could, followed the little boy's cries. He had trouble negotiating the stairs, Cody's distress adding to his own growing panic. He burst into the nursery, hurried to the crib, his ears hurting from the noise the little boy emitted.

Where was his grandmother?

He set aside his crutch and grabbed the tiny, upset bundle of baby. Cody arched his back, his fists batting the air, screeching with eyes scrunched shut as Grady tried to lift him out of the crib.

Grady wobbled on his feet, trying to hold the squirming child. Cody turned away again, screaming even louder, and Grady lost his footing.

He was going down.

He twisted, shifting his center of balance so that Cody would land on top of him.

Excruciating pain drilled through Grady's

thigh, up his back and into his head as he landed hard on his bad leg. Cody let out another squawk.

Grady rode out the waves of agony, breathing slowly, then he lifted his head to see Cody staring at him, finally quiet. Thankfully he was unhurt.

"Grady. What happened?" Grandma Mamie burst into the room and hurried to Grady's side, taking Cody from him. "How did you fall? Are you okay?"

Grady sucked in another breath, the pain slowly subsiding. "I'm fine," he said, though he felt anything but. His leg felt as though it was on fire and his head as if someone had pounded a nail through it.

Mamie cradled Cody on her hip and hooked her arm through Grady's as if to help him up.

"Please, don't," he protested, gently pulling away. "I need to get up on my own." Besides, he didn't want to pull Mamie down with him in case he lost his balance again.

He rolled to one side, got his good knee under him and, using the bars of the crib, pulled himself upright. A red-hot poker jabbed him again and he faltered.

"You're not okay. You're hurt."

"I'm fine," he ground out as the pain subsided, leaving in its wake the residue of humiliation and embarrassment. Couldn't even pick up a baby out of his bed. How was he supposed to keep up the workload created by the ranch? Not everything could be given to the hired hands. He carefully got his balance and reached for his crutch.

"You look pale," Mamie murmured, still hovering, her hand raised as if to help him again.

"How's Cody?" He turned the attention to the little boy.

Mamie shifted her gaze to the little boy, now lying still in her arms. "He seems okay."

"Should we bring him to see Dr. Tyler?" The pediatrician would have a better idea if Cody was sick or not, Grady figured.

"You're the one I'm worried about."

Grady grabbed his crutch, wishing he didn't feel so helpless. "You don't need to worry about me. Vanessa should have been here to take care of the baby."

"I think we need to confront her," his grandmother said, a note of steel in her voice that Grady remembered all too well as a child. Mamie Stillwater might come across as easygoing but when push came to shove, she could be as immovable as half of Texas.

"When she comes back we'll deal with this once and for all," Grady said, massaging the back of his neck with one hand, trying to ease away the tension that seemed to be his constant companion.

Mamie looked down at the baby reaching for her glasses. "We know for sure he is a Stillwater.

I think we need to know for sure if he is a Vane. I think we need to do a DNA test on her."

"That would either corroborate her story or rule her out," he said.

But if Vanessa was the mother, they needed to have a sit-down with her about her responsibilities. She needed to take on more and not count on Mamie.

But if the test proved she wasn't Cody's mother, that left them with the troubling question of who was.

Grady rubbed his head, the pain there battling the pain in his leg.

You should let Chloe help you. Maybe she can do something for you?

Grady held that thought a moment, trying to imagine himself showing exactly how vulnerable he was in front of a woman he hadn't been able to stop thinking about.

He couldn't. He just couldn't.

Chapter Three

"So what are you going to do now for employment?" Lucy Benson took a sip of her coffee, her green gaze flicking around the patrons of Maggie's Coffee Shop.

The place was busy. Abigail Bardera zipped around carrying plates of steaming food, her long black hair pulled back in a glossy ponytail. Maggie poured coffee, helping take orders.

"Blunt much?" Amelia said with a note of reprimand, shaking her head at their friend, her blond curly hair bouncing on her shoulders.

"May as well lay it out on the table," Lucy said.

As soon as Lucy had heard about Chloe's situation, she'd called Amelia and insisted that they take Chloe out for coffee and pie at Maggie's.

"I don't know." Chloe poked her fork at the flaky apple pie Amelia had insisted she order. "I already talked to Maggie about working here, but that's a no-go." She fought down the too-familiar sense of panic at the thought of being unemployed.

She was supposed to have worked today but yesterday Dr. Schuster had told her to consider Thursday her last day. He had hoped it would give her some more time to find a job.

"Would you move back to Fort Worth?" Amelia asked, her tone concerned.

"Too many bad memories there, though if there's work there I might. To coin a phrase that has been the mantra of my life lately, beggars can't be choosers." Her stomach roiled again at the thought of having to leave. Start over. Find her balance again on her own.

Just her and her baby.

"I know things are bad when you're resorting to clichés." Lucy tucked her short blonde hair behind her ear, her eyes holding Chloe's as if trying to encourage her.

"My life is a cliché," Chloe grumped, then waved the complaint off. "Sorry. I shouldn't whine. It's just getting hard to find the silver lining."

"Well, every silver lining has a cloud," Lucy quipped. "And it's not your fault Jeremy cheated on you. I always knew he was a jerk."

If she only knew how much of a jerk.

Chloe cut off that thought. She didn't want to give Jeremy any space in her mind. Bad enough he didn't want to have anything to do with the baby she carried. And that he had disappeared after emptying out the bank account.

"At least you're not going to tell me I told you so," Chloe said. "You did warn me not to marry in haste."

"Are you not listening to Lucy?" Amelia said with a warning wag of her finger. "You're spouting clichés again."

A sudden burst of laughter at one end of the café caught Chloe's attention. Carson Thorn stood by a table of people, laughing at something one of them had said.

"Carson looks more relaxed lately," Chloe said.

"Getting reunited with his childhood sweetheart probably helped mitigate the stress of all these thefts that he and the other members of the league have been dealing with," Lucy said with a wry tone. "Nice that there can be happy endings in this town." She shot a glance over at Amelia. "And speaking of happy endings, how are you and Finn getting on?"

To Chloe's surprise, her friend blushed. She hadn't thought spunky and vivacious Amelia knew how to blush.

"Quite well. Making plans."

Lucy sighed. "Like I said, I'm happy for happy endings."

Chloe gave her apple pie another stab, wishing

she could hope for a happy ending in her particular story. She doubted any man would want to take her on now.

"You're looking pensive," Lucy said. "I thought that was my job?"

Chloe knew Lucy had been on edge the past few months, the pressure of all the thefts in the area making her extratense and vigilant. "That's why I'm trying not to complain. I know you're under a lot of stress lately."

As well, Chloe wasn't ready to divulge her secret to Lucy and Amelia. Not while she was still adjusting to the idea, trying to figure out what shape her life would take.

"This string of thefts has been a frustrating nightmare." Lucy looked as if she wanted to say more when someone stopped by their table.

"Good afternoon, ladies." Mamie Stillwater's smile encompassed the three of them, the light from the windows beside them glinting off her glasses and polishing her gray hair. "I'm sorry to interrupt, but is it possible to talk to you alone, Chloe?"

"I have to head out right away," Lucy said, giving Chloe a look she interpreted as "tell me everything later."

"And I have to meet Finn to go over some wedding plans," Amelia said, getting up as well and dropping a few bills on the table. "This should cover everything."

Chloe was about to protest but Amelia just shook her head and gave her a bright smile. "And now we'll leave the two of you alone."

"Thanks so much."

"We'll talk more later." Amelia walked toward the entrance, but Lucy stopped by the table where Carson stood. Chloe guessed she would be asking him if he had heard about more thefts or people receiving anonymous gifts.

"You know we have little Cody at our house," Mamie said as she sat down in the chair Lucy had vacated. "My niece Eva used to be his nanny, but she's married now. I have a cook but Martha Rose went to go help her mother who broke her leg, which means I can't spend as much time with Cody as I'd like. And Grady was supposed to be doing physical therapy with you and he isn't."

She stopped there and Chloe waited, not sure where Mamie was going with all of this.

Mamie gave her a tight smile. "I'm sorry, but I overheard Dr. Schuster talking to you about your job, or lack of one..."

"How did you know about that?"

Mamie paused, her hands folded, fingers tapping against each other as she gave Chloe an apologetic look. "I didn't mean to listen in. I was in the room behind you when I heard him say that."

Chloe's cheeks warmed. A witness to her firing. But Mamie seemed genuinely sorry and Chloe guessed it wasn't her fault. Dr. Schuster should have been more discreet.

"Again, I'm sorry," Mamie continued. "But what I was wondering, given that we have Cody to take care of and Grady who won't go to therapy, would you be willing to work for me? I thought if you were actually at the house, Grady would be more amenable to participate in his recovery. And, truthfully, I need someone to help us with the little boy."

"I thought Vanessa was staying with you?" Chloe asked.

Mamie shot a look around the café, as if checking to see if anyone was listening, then leaned closer, concern etched on her features. "I know she's your stepsister, but truthfully, she doesn't seem to want to spend the time with Cody that he needs. It would help us out a lot if you would be willing to work for me."

Chloe wasn't sure she wanted to stay in the same house as Vanessa. It was too easy to recall the stinging comments her stepsister had steadily lobbed her way when they'd lived together and how Vanessa had often put her down in front of her friends.

But the cold facts of her life made her shelve her pride. Truth was she needed a job.

"So how long would you need me for?"

"Not sure." Mamie sighed. "As long as Ben is in a coma and Grady is handicapped by his injury…" Her voice trailed off and as she pressed her lips together Chloe felt a flash of sympathy for the poor woman. It must have been so difficult to see her grandsons both dealing with difficulties as well as deal with the extra strain of taking care of an unexpected great-grandbaby.

And then there was Vanessa.

"All right. I'll do it. When do you want me to start?"

"Whenever you're done at the hospital."

"Yesterday was my last day."

"Can you come now?"

The weariness in her voice, plus the light touch of Mamie's hand on Chloe's, made her stifle her objections and give in. "I'll come today."

"Excellent. Thank you so much." Mamie sank back in her chair, the relief on her face palpable. "I'll go directly to the ranch and get your room ready."

"My room?"

Mamie looked taken aback. "Yes. I thought you knew. I'm sorry if I didn't make that clear. I was hoping you would be staying at the ranch overnight. To help with Cody."

Chloe sucked in a breath at the thought of having to face Grady, Vanessa and Cody all together day and night. It was a small comfort to know that Grady was not Cody's father, but that still left Vanessa and her flirtatious ways.

But a job was a job, she reminded herself. Something she needed until she could figure out her next move.

"Okay. I'll pack my things and meet you at the ranch."

"Why don't I go with you and we can drive back with each other? You remember where the ranch is, right?"

Too clearly, Chloe thought, remembering a trip she had made with Vanessa to the Stillwater ranch. The day she'd first seen her stepsister kissing the boy she had cared for so deeply.

"Hush now, Cody. Please go to sleep." Grady stood by the crib rubbing one large hand over the baby's back in a vain effort to get him to settle down. Vanessa was still gone and his grandmother had left on some mysterious trip to town.

Cody had been crying for an hour now. Grady felt more out of his league than he had that time he and his fellow soldiers had been pinned down by crossfire. At least then he had training to fall back on.

He had no training to deal with a kid who wouldn't settle down.

He should call Eva. Or her husband. They

would know. He was just about to do that when he heard voices. And with relief he grabbed his crutch and stumped over to the door to listen. Was Vanessa back?

He heard footsteps coming up the stairs, and a figure rounded the corner. She was slim with long wavy brown hair spilling over one shoulder of a plaid shirt tucked into snug blue jeans. Beautiful and sweet looking.

Grady blinked. Chloe? What was she doing here?

His grandmother materialized behind her, a grin taking over her face. "Isn't this wonderful?" Mamie said. "Chloe has agreed to come help us out."

"And from the sounds of things, I better get to work," she said, giving him a vague smile. "Is he hungry?"

"No. He just had a bottle."

Chloe gave him a tight nod and hurried past him into Cody's room.

Grady looked from her to his grandmother, who stood in front of him looking mighty pleased with herself.

"What is going on?" he whispered, moving her away from the door so Chloe wouldn't overhear them.

The cries from the nursery stilled and he heard Chloe's gentle murmur as she settled the baby.

"We said we needed to do something about Cody. Chloe lost her job at the hospital. And you need therapy and you won't go. Martha Rose is gone. So I thought this was a perfect solution for all of us. Chloe can help us with Cody and she can work with you, leaving me free to help with the cooking and where I'm needed. Win, win."

Grady could only stare at his grandmother, trying to absorb what she had just told him.

"Chloe? Do physical therapy with me? Here?"

"One question at a time," his grandmother said, wagging her finger at him, a definitely mischievous smile on her face. "Chloe. Yes. And yes, I do want her to do physical therapy here. You know that is what you need to do. I can see by the grimace on your face and by the way you walk. It's only getting worse and, I fear, will continue to get worse. You have to take care of yourself."

Grady clenched his jaw, knowing his grandmother was right but not sure he wanted Chloe seeing his helplessness.

"You are the only man I have around," his grandmother said, playing a last, devastating card. "I need you to help me as much as possible."

Surely there had to be another way?

"I agree that we need help with Cody," he conceded. "As for the rest, well, we'll see."

And that was all he was giving her.

"That's fine," his grandmother said with a bright smile. "One step at a time."

He watched her leave, eyes narrowed, feeling as though he had just agreed to something he would regret.

He returned to the nursery to check on Cody.

Chloe stood in profile to him, rocking the baby, such a maternal smile on her face that Grady's knees grew weak. This was what a mother looked like, he thought, taking in the sight of this beautiful woman holding this baby so tenderly.

"I think he's asleep," Chloe whispered, her attention still focused on Cody. As she gently laid him down, Cody started, his hands shooting into the air, then as Chloe stroked his face he settled again, his breathing growing deep and even. It was amazing, he thought, envious of her ability to soothe the child, yet so grateful she could.

She gave his face another stroke of her hand and stepped away.

"We can go now," she said, keeping her voice down.

She left ahead of Grady and he gently closed the door behind him. Together they walked down the hallway.

"Thanks so much for your help," Grady said, following her to the top of the stairs. "I didn't know what to do anymore. You seem to be a natural mother."

She stopped there, her hand gripping the railing, her knuckles white, a look of fear on her face.

Had he said something wrong? Hurt her in some way?

She turned, folded her arms over her stomach. "Before we see your grandmother, I need to know how comfortable you are with working with me. I don't think my coming to help you was your idea."

Grady held her steady gaze, appreciating her straightforward honesty, such a refreshing change from her manipulative stepsister.

And that's not the only thing you appreciate about her, a perfidious voice teased.

He shook it off, his injury a grim reminder of why she was here and what he had to offer someone like her.

"It wasn't my idea. For now, let's just leave it at you taking care of Cody."

"But I saw your file. You need to keep working on your mobility."

"I will. I just don't have time yet. I've got the ranch and the program Ben set up to oversee. If Ben hadn't been so foolhardy..." He stopped himself there. Chloe may be employed here, but she didn't need to know all the ins and outs of their lives. "Anyhow, let's go have some coffee with my grandma, because I'm sure she's getting some ready."

"I have your assessment. Dr. Schuster gave that to me so we could start from there."

"You don't give up, do you?"

"One of the characteristics of being a physical therapist. A quiet stubbornness."

He laughed at that, glancing sidelong at her. But he didn't look away and neither did Chloe. Their eyes held and a peculiar feeling of awareness rose up. An echo of older emotions she had once created.

She swallowed and he saw her take a quick breath.

Did she feel it, too?

Then he took a step closer and his foot caught on the carpet of the hallway. He faltered, thankfully just for a moment, as reality shot down any foolish thoughts he might have entertained.

She turned away, went down the stairs, quickly outpacing him.

And as he made his slow, painful way behind her he was reminded once again the foolishness of allowing himself to feel anything for any woman.

The only trouble was Chloe wasn't just any woman. At one time he had cared for her. But she'd given him no indication that she returned his feelings. And then Vanessa had come along. After that, the war.

Now his life was a tangle of obligations and

unmet expectations. He knew he had to be realistic. He couldn't offer her anything. Not anymore.

"So you took the job?" Lucy was asking.

Holding her cell phone close to her ear, Chloe sat back on the bed of the room Mamie Stillwater had shown her to. It was off the nursery and a full floor away from the room Grady stayed in, which was a good thing.

Her room was lovely, though. Painted a soft aqua, trimmed with white casings, the room was large, cozy and welcoming. A chair and small reading table were tucked into a corner beside an expansive bay window that overlooked the ranch. The bed filled another corner, and a small walk-in closet and en suite gave her all the privacy she needed. It was lavish and luxurious compared to the cramped furnished apartment she had been renting.

"I didn't have much choice," Chloe said.

"Won't hurt to see Grady every day," Lucy teased.

"It's strictly professional," Chloe said, trying not to let the image of Vanessa fawning over Grady get to her. "Besides, I don't know how much one-on-one time I'll be spending with him. He seems intent on avoiding therapy."

"If he's as stubborn as his brother, you've got your work cut out for you."

Lucy sighed lightly and Chloe sensed her friend's extra stress. "You sound tired. Have there been more thefts?"

"Another one at the Cutler ranch last night," Lucy said. "Some ATVs and a horse. I'm getting worried that this is more organized than people think."

Chloe twisted a thread from the cuff of her worn blue jeans around her finger. "Do you have any leads?"

"None. Though something has been puzzling me greatly. The Stillwater ranch is the only large ranch that doesn't seem to have had any thefts at all. A few of the smaller ones have been avoided as well, but I'm still trying to see if there's a connection. A pattern that I can't find. I was hoping you could help me out."

"How?"

"Just keep your eyes and ears open. Maybe get closer to Mamie. I don't know."

"And report anything I might hear back to you."

"Please."

"Okay. I'll see what I can find out." She stifled the feeling of guilt that accompanied her statement. She was thankful for the job and she didn't want to take advantage of that.

Yet Lucy was her friend. And she would be helping her and the community out.

"I should go. Mamie said that dinner was in a few minutes."

"Hey, thanks for doing this for me," Lucy said. "I appreciate any help I can get."

Chloe said goodbye, then made quick work of changing her flannel shirt and pants for a clean pair of blue jeans and an aqua silk shirt. She brushed her hair and, giving in to an impulse, applied some blush and mascara.

For Grady?

Chloe lifted her chin and looked at her reflection in the mirror. For herself, she thought, clipping part of her hair back with a couple of bobby pins. She couldn't allow herself to think of Grady. Not while she carried another man's baby.

Before she could give in to doing any more primping, she left. She paused at the door of the nursery, but all was silent.

She hurried down the stairs. However, no one was in the kitchen by the table, so she followed the conversation to the formal dining room.

Grady sat at one end of the table and as she came in, Vanessa got up from her end and sat by him. As if trying to show Chloe where things stood. Grady didn't seem interested, however, which gave her a small encouragement. He looked up, struggling to stand.

Vanessa frowned at Grady. "Just relax. It's only

Chloe." Then Vanessa's icy glance ticked over her. "That's an interesting look."

Chloe's heart turned over as she mentally compared Vanessa's silky dress and perfect makeup with her own clothes. She had thought she looked okay, but now she felt drab and dull. She didn't think she needed to dress for dinner.

Vanessa gave her a wry look. "Well, I guess it's too late to change."

Chloe wished she could ignore her stepsister's dismissive attitude.

"I think you look great," Grady said.

His words shouldn't have made her feel as good as they did.

Mamie, who wore plain dress pants and a shirt partially covered by her apron, entered and set a platter of ham beside bowls of steaming potatoes and salads and vegetables. At least she looked more casual.

"Do you need any help?" Chloe asked her.

Mamie waved off her offer as she removed her apron and laid it on a side table. "No, dear. This is the last plate. Please sit down." Mamie pulled a chair away from the table, leaving the only empty spot available opposite Vanessa but beside Grady. Chloe sat down and plucked her napkin out of the ring, ignoring Vanessa's calculating look.

"Is Cody sleeping?" Vanessa asked, leaning close to Grady, as if staking her claim on him. Again.

"He is."

"Poor baby. I think I wore him out playing with him," Vanessa said with a smug smile.

"Well, here we are all together," Mamie said, but Chloe caught a strained note in her voice.

"One big happy family," Vanessa chimed in, and reached for the salad bowl. "Grady, can I serve you some salad?"

"I thought we would pray first," Mamie said.

"Oh. Right." Vanessa fluttered her hands in an "I'm silly" gesture, then gave Grady another arched look. "I always forget."

Just before Chloe lowered her head, however, she couldn't help a glance Grady's way and was disconcerted to see him looking directly at her.

Then she felt a tinge of nausea, a remnant of what she had been struggling with the first four months of her pregnancy, a reminder, and she quickly drew her gaze away.

Mamie prayed a blessing on the food, asking as well for some solution to the thefts, thanks for family and another request for Ben's recovery.

Chloe kept her head bowed a moment, adding her own prayer to stay focused on her work here and not be distracted by inappropriate feelings better left buried.

"I heard there was another theft at the McKay spread," Vanessa said, her voice bright, her ex-

pression holding a forced gaiety when Mamie
was done.

"I'm sure Byron was upset about that," Mamie
replied.

"And you guys haven't had anything stolen?"
Vanessa asked, taking a tiny bite of her salad.

"Not yet, thankfully." Grady handed the platter of ham in front of him to Chloe. "Would you
like some?"

Chloe felt a start of surprise, her mind as much
on the job Lucy had asked her to do here on the
Stillwater ranch as trying not to be so aware of
Grady sitting only a few feet from her. "Sure.
Thank you." As she took the plate, however, she
caught Vanessa's narrowed gaze.

"That's interesting," Vanessa said, dragging
out the word, larding it with innuendo. "Makes
one wonder if it's not that foster girl you've got
working here who could be behind the thefts.
Maddy something or other. She doesn't come
from the best family. Sort of like Chloe here.
Having an alcoholic father can't be easy."

"I think that's enough," Grady said, a harsh
note of reprimand in his voice.

"Well, it's true." Vanessa stabbed at her salad.
"About Maddy anyway."

The supper conversation limped along after
that. Vanessa picked at her food, shooting glances
over at Grady, who steadfastly ignored her. All

the while Chloe was far too aware of Grady's eyes on her and of Vanessa's occasional glower. The tension was noticeable and Chloe was thankful when the meal was finally over.

Chloe declined dessert as she got up from the table, saying she should check on Cody.

As she hurried up the stairs, second thoughts nipped at her heels. She shouldn't have taken this job. How long could she put up with Vanessa and her judgmental attitude and snide comments?

But even as those questions plagued her, she knew Grady's presence created the tighter tension.

She slipped into the nursery and stood by the crib, her arms wrapped tightly around her midsection. She could feel a bump that she knew would start to show soon. For now, however, she could still wear her regular clothes.

And what will you do when you can't?

She doubted Mamie would let her go. After all, they had taken in Vanessa, who was an unwed mother. She doubted Mamie would judge her.

But even as that thought formulated, she thought of how Grady avoided Vanessa in spite of her flirting. She wondered if his attitude toward her had something to do with Vanessa's situation—being an unwed mother.

Cody lay on his side, arms curled up, looking utterly adorable.

A confusing brew of emotions stirred within her as she pressed her hand to her abdomen in a protective gesture.

"He's sleeping?"

Grady's voice from the doorway made her jump. She spun around just as he joined her by the crib.

"He looks so peaceful," Grady said, leaning on the rail as if to get a closer look. Then Grady looked over at her and gave her a cautious smile. "I'm sorry about what Vanessa said over dinner."

"You don't have to apologize," Chloe said. "I heard a lot worse growing up."

"I keep forgetting you two are sisters."

"Stepsisters," Chloe reminded him. "And Vanessa only lived at the ranch for a while."

"If I may ask, what made her mother leave?"

Chloe's conscience fought with a desire to tell him the bare truth. There hadn't been enough money for Etta Vane. The ranch hadn't been as prosperous as she had thought.

"I don't think ranch life suited Etta. Or Vanessa. The reality was a shock for them."

"Somehow she seems to like our place just fine," Grady said.

Because there's money here.

But she dismissed the thought. The little boy sleeping in the crib in front of her was her stepsister's reason for returning. As was the man standing beside her.

"I...I should go," she said.

To her dismay, she felt Grady's hand on her shoulder as she straightened. The warmth of his fingers through her shirt sent a tingle of awareness down her spine; the glint of his eyes in the soft glow of the night-light created an unexpected and unwelcome attraction. "Don't take to heart what Vanessa said to you."

"I'm used to it," Chloe said, struggling to keep the breathless tone out of her voice.

"Was it hard? Living with her?"

Chloe shrugged, then gave him a faint smile. "I just wished we could have been closer. But maybe there's time now that she's here."

He held her gaze, his expression earnest. "I feel as if I need to tell you because you're working here now, with Cody, that while I know I'm not his father, neither do I believe she's Cody's mother."

"What?" Vanessa's screech from the doorway broke into the moment. "How dare you say things like that? I'm his mother, Grady Stillwater." She rounded on Chloe. "You were feeding him some lies, weren't you? You always were jealous of me. You're so plain and dumpy. You could never compete with me. You and your useless father. I can't believe my mother even married him. He was a lousy rancher and a crippled drunk."

Chloe fought her inborn urge to defend her father. It wasn't his fault his grandfather hadn't left as much money as Etta had hoped. It wasn't his fault he'd been injured when he had his ATV accident.

"Vanessa, that's enough," Grady snapped.

"Enough of what?" Vanessa said, rounding on him. "You don't need to stand up for her. You need to face the truth."

"If we're talking about truth, it should be an easy matter to get a DNA test done on you," Cody said, his voice surprisingly calm. "That should give us the truth about who Cody's biological mother is."

Vanessa paled at that, glancing from Chloe to Grady, her eyes wide. "I can't believe you doubt me. I can't believe you think I'm not his mother…" Her voice drifted off and with another accusing glare at Chloe, Vanessa spun around and strode away.

Grady blew out a sigh as he shoved his hands through his hair. "Again. Sorry about that," he said. "I shouldn't have confronted her. Made her say those things about you and your father."

Chloe looked down at Cody, who lay fast asleep and blissfully unaware of the drama unfolding in his nursery. "I'm just glad he didn't wake up" was all she could manage.

Grady touched her again and she turned to him.

"You always were a pure, sweet person," he said.

Once again her former attraction to him bubbled to the surface.

Then Chloe felt another flicker of nausea.

She pulled back, turned away from him, the feeling a stark reminder of the main reason she couldn't encourage him. Couldn't be with him.

The child she carried. The child conceived with her ex-husband.

Chapter Four

"Have you seen Vanessa this morning?" Mamie asked, beating some eggs in a bowl.

Grady looked up from the laptop he had propped on the eating bar of the kitchen. Ben had all the livestock records, all the bookkeeping, all the information on the Future Ranchers in files on the computer, and Grady had been poring over them in an attempt to get up to speed.

"No. I thought she was sleeping in."

"I had to get something from the closet in her room and knocked on the door but when I opened it, there was no one in the room. Her bed was empty." Mamie beat the eggs, the frown on her face clearly expressing her concern. "I'm glad we hired Chloe to help us."

"I am, too." Grady's thoughts skipped back to that moment last night in the nursery. Seeing Chloe standing by the crib, smiling down at Cody, had created a mixture of emotions he had a hard time processing. He knew he was attracted to her. And he sensed something building between them.

But all it took was one shift of his weight on his leg, one look at the crutch to remind him of the foolishness of letting these feelings take over. He wasn't the man he once was.

No. She deserved better than this.

Just as he made this resolution, she came into the kitchen, Cody cuddled up against her. The baby still wore his sleeper. He was rubbing his eyes, his rosy cheeks holding the imprint of one of his chubby hands, his blanket tucked under one arm.

Grady felt a warmth kindle in him at the sight.

Trouble was he knew it wasn't the sight of Cody that caused it, but the woman holding him.

"Good morning, Chloe," he said, giving her a wary smile.

She just nodded at him, suddenly impersonal. Clearly he had stepped over some line she had drawn last night.

"Hey, sweetie." Mamie reached for the boy, beaming at the sight of Cody holding out his arms to her in answer. "Did you have a good sleep?"

"He woke up once early this morning," Chloe said. "I went to see what was wrong and Vanessa was in the nursery. I thought she was picking him up, but she just stood by his crib and then left. I found this on his night table when I got Cody this morning." She tugged an envelope out of the back pocket of her blue jeans and handed it to him.

Grady frowned as he slit it open and pulled a single piece of paper out.

"Dear Stillwaters," he read aloud. "I decided to leave. You were right. Cody's not my kid. But I'm guessing he is Grady's, because that's what you Stillwaters are like. Love 'em and leave 'em. Have a good life. Vanessa."

"So why did she write that now?" Mamie asked, her fingers pressed against her lips.

Grady folded up the letter and put it in the envelope. "I told her that a simple DNA test could easily prove if she was the mother or not. I'm guessing she knew we would find out the truth." He thought of the cruel things Vanessa had thrown at Chloe as she'd left, yet was thankful Chloe wouldn't have lingering doubts about his relationship with Vanessa.

But Chloe was filling up a bottle with formula for Cody and not paying attention to him. Clearly that moment he thought they had shared was over.

Not that he blamed her.

"When Cody is down for his morning nap, I thought we could start doing some therapy," Chloe said to Grady, her entire focus on getting the milk into the bottle. Obviously the job required intense concentration.

"I need to talk to the kids this morning. Maddy Coles is coming to do some work with our horse trainer."

Chloe gave him a sharp look. "Is Maddy the girl who Vanessa referred to?"

"Yes." Grady ground out the single word, still angry at Vanessa's insinuations.

"Vanessa can be thoughtless," Chloe said, screwing the lid on the baby bottle. "I don't think she always realizes what she is saying."

"I can't believe you can defend her," Grady said. "Especially after what she said about your father. Her comments were uncalled for and unkind."

Chloe's gaze shot to his, the surprise in her eyes shifting to gratitude as she took Cody from his grandmother. "Thanks for that. Dad was… He had his difficulties."

One of them being Vanessa's mother, Grady was sure. "Your father was a good man who had some bad things happen to him. And I should know. My father had his own issues after his injuries."

"Thanks for understanding." Chloe's smile wormed its way past his defenses.

"Did you want some breakfast, Chloe?" Mamie

asked, dipping bread into the egg mixture. "I'm making French toast."

"That sounds wonderful," Chloe said. "I'll feed Cody and then I can help you."

"You just sit down and take care of that little boy," Mamie said, patting Cody on his cheek and giving Chloe a warm smile. "I'll take care of breakfast."

Wasn't too hard to see that his grandmother liked Chloe, Grady thought. Most likely one of the reasons she'd hired her.

Against his will his mind returned to last night. To that brief connection he and Chloe had shared. And then to her sudden turn away from him. It was a vivid reminder of his situation.

He finished his breakfast and got up.

"I'm going out to the barn," he said, balancing his plate and mug in one hand as he maneuvered past the table to the kitchen counter.

"Will you be coming back to the house later on?" Chloe asked.

"For lunch, maybe." Grady knew she referred to the therapy she wanted to do. But he didn't want to spend more time with her than he had to. Didn't want to be reminded even more clearly of his shortcomings.

"Do you mind if I go out to the barns?" Chloe stood in the doorway of a small room just off the master bedroom where Mamie slept. The older woman was bent over a sewing machine sitting to one side of the room. She was making quilt squares from what Chloe could tell.

The older woman looked up and pushed her glasses back down on her nose. "No. That's not a problem."

"Cody is down for his afternoon nap. He'll be good for at least two and a half hours."

"Are you going to try to talk to Grady?"

"*Try* being the operative word," Chloe said with a wry smile.

Mamie sat back in her chair and folded her arms over her chest. "I think you'll be able to charm him," she said with a twinkle in her eye.

"I was hoping to set up downstairs in the recreation room, if that was okay? I noticed some exercise equipment in there that I might be able to use."

"That's fine. Do you need any other equipment for him?"

"Some mats and foam rollers once I do my own assessment. I've already spoken with Salma, the physical therapist at the hospital. She said she would be willing to rent some of what I need, if that's okay with you."

"Whatever you need," Mamie said with a wave of her hand. "You just let me know."

"Thanks." Chloe was about to leave when Mamie spoke up again.

"He's a good man," Mamie said, her voice almost pleading. "I know the war has changed him. I know he feels less of a man than he was. He's pulled into himself, but deep down I know he's still the same honorable and loving man he was when he left. And you know that he and your stepsister were never…"

"I know and I understand," Chloe said, holding up one hand to stop the dear woman's defense of her grandson. It was hard to listen to because she spoke Chloe's own thoughts aloud.

Last night, after she and Grady had shared that moment in the nursery, she had lain awake for too long, one hand resting on her stomach where her baby grew, the other on her chest to ease the sorrow in her heart.

"I want to ask another question," Mamie said. "And you can say no if you're uncomfortable, but we'll be attending church tomorrow—"

"I'd love to come," Chloe said.

"Wonderful." Mamie gave her a bright smile, then turned back to her sewing.

Chloe grabbed a jacket and headed out the door. As she left the shelter of the porch, a chill wind snatched her breath away and tossed her hair around her face. She shivered and hurried down the path toward what she guessed was the horse barn.

Muted voices echoed down the long alleyway, her footfalls softened by the wooden floor. Chloe inhaled the scent of the barn, so familiar it created an ache. While her father had never been able to afford a facility such as this, the old barn they'd used for the horses had held the same smells—oil, leather, old wood and horses.

A horse nickered at her as she passed, poking its head over the top of a stall.

Chloe smiled at the mare, took a moment to pet her, then reluctantly left, following the voices to the end of the barn. She turned a corner to a large area that was roofed in but open to the weather.

Grady held the halter of a palomino, stroking its neck while a heavyset man with a shock of white hair was bent over one of the hooves he had tucked between his legs. Chloe recognized Saul Bateman, the local farrier and one-time friend of her father. The sight of him hurt. Though Saul and her father had been friends, Saul hadn't attended her father's funeral and she hadn't seen him until now.

A young girl—Maddy Coles, Chloe guessed—stood beside Saul, her head tilted to watch him work. She was small, slender with a darker complexion and black hair. A pair of earbuds dangled from a cord hanging out of the chest pocket of her worn denim jacket.

"You might want to put that fancy new iPod away before you drop it on the ground," Grady was saying.

"Sorry, Mr. Stillwater," she said with a shrug and a grin. "I don't want to lose it."

"I still find it interesting that iPod and all that other stuff just showed up at your place," Grady said. "Did you ever find out who brought it?"

Chloe stopped where she was, remembering the buzz about how Maddy's foster parents, Judd and Ann Derring, had received some cattle, farm equipment and some clothes for the children, as well as the iPod Maddy now tucked back into her pocket. Maybe Maddy would say something Chloe could pass on to Lucy.

"Not a clue," Maddy said. "Though it was exciting. Timmy hasn't had his nose out of those books since he got them."

"I think it's weird," Saul commented as he dug into the hoof of the horse. "Weird and wrong to steal from people. Then to give other people gifts. Can't figure out why Lucy hasn't found whoever is doing it."

"It can't be easy. It seems to be so random," Grady added. He turned back to Saul. "So why don't you tell Maddy what you're doing, Saul?"

Clearly Grady was done talking about the thefts and wanted to move on.

"Of course." Saul shifted his weight to accommodate the sudden movement of the horse. "You need to make sure you get all the dirt and snow out of the hoof before we trim the hooves and then shoe them," he said to Maddy. "We use this hoof pick for cleaning."

The horse Grady held looked up and whickered at Chloe. Grady glanced back, frowning when he saw her. "Hey, you," he said with a nod. "Cody sleeping?"

"Which is why I'm here," she said, wishing his frown and dismissive attitude didn't bother her as much as they did. "I thought we'd get started on your exercises today."

"I'm kind of busy right now," he muttered, turning back to the horse.

Saul looked up and gave Chloe a half smile. "Hey, girl. How you doing?"

"I'm good."

"I heard Vanessa is gone."

"Yes."

"I'm sorry about the funeral."

Chloe only nodded her acknowledgment of Saul's comment. It had hurt that her father's old friend hadn't attended, but she suspected it had much to do with the falling out the two of them had had over his marrying Etta and the consequences thereof.

Saul had warned her father not to get involved with Etta Vane. But her father, lonely and grieving, had jumped too quickly into another relationship and cut Saul out of his life. "And I'm sorry," he said, holding her gaze, his expression full of regret. "Sorry about your father. He didn't deserve what happened to him. That Etta woman was pure poison."

"Well, Vanessa is gone and I doubt she'll be back," Chloe said. "But for now I have work to do. Grady, are you able to come?" She didn't want to talk about her father and the circumstances of his life. He hadn't been all that happy in this life; she knew he was much happier now.

"I can hold Charger and watch Mr. Bateman work so you can go," Maddy offered, her voice eager.

"It's okay. I'm fine," Grady said. "Just keep going."

Chloe tried hard not to sigh, but his reluctance to let her help him was annoying.

"I'm not going anywhere," Chloe said.

"Great. You hold Charger still while I get the next horse."

"Okay." She took the halter rope and almost laughed at the surprise on his face. She wasn't leaving him alone until he agreed to start therapy.

"Fine. Then I'll get the next horse."

"Sure. You do that."

He frowned at her as if wondering if she was poking fun of him, which she was. He grabbed his crutch and headed out into the paddock.

"You taking care of Cody now?" Maddy asked, carefully digging at the hoof with the pick under Saul's tutelage. "I thought you worked at the hospital."

"The job was only temporary and so Mrs. Stillwater offered me a job here."

Maddy bent over and the earbuds of her iPod fell out of her pocket again. "Whoops," she said, tucking them back in.

Chloe thought of Lucy's request to keep an eye on things at the ranch. "Have you received any other anonymous gifts?" she asked, hoping she sounded more casual than she felt.

"No. Just this stuff." Maddy shrugged and buttoned the pocket this time. "Makes me feel kind of special and creeped out at the same time."

"Have any of your friends at school gotten anything?"

"No." Maddy grunted and dug at the hoof with her pick.

Saul shot her a puzzled look and Chloe decided to stop her questioning. No need to draw attention to herself.

The horse she held nickered and she glanced

back to see Grady trying to lead the other horse with one hand and handle his crutch with the other. The horse he was leading balked, his crutch clattered to the floor and he stumbled, grabbing the horse by the mane to right himself.

Chloe took a step toward him to help, then heard Saul clear his throat as if warning her.

She caught his look then turned away, pretending she hadn't seen what had happened, though it bothered her deeply to see this proud man so helpless.

Maddy, intent on getting every last bit of dirt out of the horse's hoof, thankfully didn't know what was going on.

A few moments later Grady joined them, his crutch under his arm again, leading the horse. "I'll tie him up here," he said, breathing heavily.

Chloe fought down a beat of frustration. Why couldn't this man see he needed her help?

But until he agreed, she could do nothing.

"I think we're done with Charger here," Saul said to Maddy. "I need to trim the hooves, but I'll have to do that on my own."

Just then a noise behind them drew Chloe's attention. Mamie walked toward them holding Cody.

"I'm sorry," Chloe said, feeling suddenly guilty for spending time out here. She held up Charger's halter rope. "Can someone take him? I need to get Cody."

"I'll hold the rope. You can go," Maddy said.

"I just came out to tell you that I got a call from the hospital," Mamie said as Chloe took Cody from her. "Ben's temperature is up. I know we talked about going tomorrow after church, but I'd like to go today."

"I'll take you," Grady said.

"I have a few things to get ready yet," Mamie said, her hands worrying each other. "If that's okay?"

"No problem."

Mamie hurried back, leaving Chloe and Grady behind.

Cody gurgled at Chloe as if he recognized her, and suddenly lurched away from her, his chubby hands flailing.

Chloe almost lost her balance, laughing as she realized Cody wanted to touch the horse. "Ah-dah. Ah-dah," he squealed in excitement.

Charger nickered, then leaned toward Cody. Chloe brought him closer and he reached out, his plump fingers batting at the horse's nose. Charger didn't so much as blink.

"I think he likes the horse," Maddy said.

"Son of his father," Saul said.

Chloe caught Grady's frown, wondering if he was thinking of Ben, Cody's father.

Grady touched the little boy's cheek with a large forefinger, the simple gesture warming Chloe's heart. Then he pulled away. "We better get going."

He walked back down the wooden alleyway. Chloe easily caught up to him and slowed her pace to match his.

Chloe glanced at the empty horse stalls. "Why don't you keep the horses in here?"

"We only use the stalls for the mares that are in foal. Sometimes we'll put a couple of the stallions in here. They cause nothing but trouble when they're out," Grady said, stopping at the stall that held the horse that had watched Chloe's progress earlier. "Hey, Sweetpea. You going to give us a nice little baby in a while?"

"She's in foal?"

"Due in a few months, as are Babe and Shiloh. Ben had them all bred to a cutting horse. He had plans to…" His voice faltered and Chloe gave into the impulse and put her hand on his shoulder in comfort. The news from the hospital must have been weighing on his mind.

To her surprise, he covered it with his own hand. Large. Warm. Welcoming.

He looked over at her and once again Chloe felt the emotions that had risen up between them that night in Cody's nursery.

Cody's squeal inserted itself into the moment, returning Chloe to reality.

"He sure seems to like horses," Chloe said, disliking how breathless she sounded.

"Like Saul said, son of his father." He looked over at her again. "I'm glad you're here to help take care of him. I know it's a job to you, but with what is going on with Ben and all, it just makes that part of our lives easier."

He gave her a careful smile and her breath quickened.

Another wave of nausea washed over her, her own reality making itself known.

"Are you okay?" Grady asked. "You look a little pale."

"I'm fine. Just tired, I think." When she'd seen the doctor before leaving Fort Worth, he hadn't seemed too concerned about the nausea. She knew she would have to make another appointment to see him soon. She could mention it then.

She walked ahead of him, her lips pressed together, holding Cody close as if to protect him.

She wondered if she was wise to encourage him to work with her and how she could maintain her distance while she did.

He was far too appealing and growing more so every day.

Chapter Five

He had forgotten about the stairs in the church.

It was Sunday morning and Grady and his grandmother had been making their way across the foyer to the sanctuary, chatting with fellow members, catching up.

And now he had to navigate these carpeted stairs.

"We can take the elevator if you want," his grandmother said with a bright note in her voice.

He knew Grandma Mamie was only being helpful. But he didn't know which would be worse—riding the elevator with dear, eighty-year-old Iva Donovan and her walker or running the risk of stumbling on the stairs.

"I can manage at home. I'm sure I can manage here."

Though as he took the first stair, he wished once again he hadn't given in to his grandmother's pleas this morning to come to church with her and Chloe. He was far too aware of the crutch he needed for support and the sympathetic glances he got from people who stopped to say hello. And he was fairly sure church would be a waste of time. He'd seen too much of the darkness of life to believe that God even cared what happened on earth.

"Are you okay?" Mamie asked, resting her hand on his arm.

He just nodded and was about to take the next step when he felt a hand on his shoulder. "Hey there," a deep voice said.

Turning, he faced Tyler Grainger, an old school friend now married to his cousin Eva.

"So glad to see you here, buddy," Tyler continued, giving him a rough, one-armed hug.

Tyler pulled back, looking into his friend's eyes as if trying to see what Grady had witnessed during his time overseas.

You'd never understand, Grady wanted to say.

"So how are you finding married life?" Mamie asked Tyler, rescuing Grady from replying to Tyler's unspoken question. Grady was thankful. He didn't want to discuss his lack of spiritual fervor in the foyer of the church. Especially not with a man who at one time had wielded strong influence in Grady's faith life.

"It's wonderful," Tyler said. "But Eva does

miss working with Cody. Though I heard you have a new nanny."

Tyler gave him a knowing look at the same time Chloe joined them. If his injury made him self-conscious, Chloe's presence only increased that emotion.

As did Tyler's discreet poke of his elbow.

"Don't you need to find Eva?" Grady asked.

"Right. I should go," Tyler said. But he gave Grady a wink and jogged up the stairs ahead of him, a vivid reminder of the physical differences between them. It was hard not to feel frustrated or less of a man.

Grady took a breath and worked his way up the stairs, Chloe right beside him, looking everywhere but at him. It seemed every moment they spent together alone only increased either his awareness of her or her retreat from him. Yesterday, when they'd stood by Ben's horse, he'd thought they had shared a small connection. Then she'd pulled back. She'd stayed home when he and his grandmother had gone to the hospital, claiming Cody was fussy. This flimsy excuse had netted him some direct questions from his grandma as to what he had done to her.

As far as he knew, he had done nothing more than cover her hand with his. Clearly a mistake, because she hadn't so much as made eye contact since then.

"Do you think Cody will be okay in the nursery?" Mamie was asking Chloe as they reached the top of the stairs and the entrance to the sanctuary.

She nodded, her gaze meeting his, then skittering away. If she was this jumpy around him after spending a few days together, why should she be surprised that he wasn't about to start physical therapy with her?

"He's settled in nicely. Of course, it's familiar to him," Chloe said, brushing at the skirt of her dress and fussing with the belt she had put on. She looked uncomfortable, as if she wished she were wearing something else.

"Well, well, look at my friend. Looking all pretty and pert in her cute dress."

Lucy Benson joined them, her bright eyes flicking from Chloe to Grady, as if he might be the reason Chloe had made this transformation.

"I told you I owned a couple of dresses," Chloe said, sounding a bit short.

Lucy patted her on the shoulder. "And now you've proved it." She glanced over at Grady. "How are things back at the ranch?"

Grady heard the subtext in her question. "No thefts yet."

Lucy just nodded. "That is intriguing. Do you have any idea why?"

"Maybe whoever is stealing feels sorry for my brother."

"Maybe. But I doubt it." Lucy gave him a cheeky look, then turned back to Chloe and frowned. "You feeling okay? You look a little green."

"And with just two comments you've effectively negated anything positive you just said," Chloe returned.

"Give with one hand, take away with the other. That's what the long arm of the law does," Lucy said with a grin. "Anyhow, I gotta go. Promised my mom I'd help her out with coffee this morning." With a flip of her blond hair and a wave of her hand, Lucy was gone.

"She's certainly a ball of fire, isn't she?" Mamie said, her tone admiring. "Always on the job."

"A bit too vigilant," Grady mumbled, not certain he liked Lucy's insinuations. He didn't know why the Stillwater ranch hadn't been robbed yet, but he guessed it was simply a matter of time until they were hit. He doubted they would be on the receiving end of any largesse on the part of the Little Horn Robin Hood.

"Can we go sit down now?" Mamie asked. "I want to make sure there's enough room for the three of us," she added, beaming as she looked from Chloe to Grady.

Grady wasn't sure he liked the satisfied look on his grandmother's face. As if seeing Chloe and Grady together made her happy. He was fairly sure she had hired Chloe for more than nannying and therapy, but he wasn't about to confront her on that.

They found their place at the end of the pew, situated in the center of the sanctuary. Grandma and Grampa Stillwater had laid claim to this spot when they'd married, and through the ebb and flow of the Stillwater family, it had become "theirs."

Grady stood aside while Grandma and then Chloe entered. Which meant he would be sitting beside Chloe.

He sat down slowly, easing his way into the seat, trying to find a place for his crutch. It fell; he bent over to pick it up and tried to lean it against the pew in front of him. Wordlessly Chloe took it and laid it on the floor at their feet.

"Thanks," he said, giving her a smile.

She returned the smile and there it was again. The awareness that sparked between them like a live thing.

This time she didn't look away as quickly.

The pianist began playing and a group of young kids came to the front. With a clang of chords from a guitarist and the piano, they started singing. Grady didn't recognize the song, but it seemed Chloe did. She sang along, her voice bright and clear and melodious.

Grady clung to the sound, the purity of her voice easing away the memories that plagued him from time to time. Reminding him of a happier time when he and his fellow soldiers had been on leave in Kandahar and had stopped to listen to a street group singing. A young girl, her voice as clear and true as Chloe's, had been singing, laughing and dancing. It had been a bright spot in that particular tour.

A day later everything had changed.

He stifled the dark thoughts, massaging his leg, clinging once again to the music to which Chloe sang along.

"'My hope is only in You, Lord, my solid cornerstone, my strength when I am weak, my help when I'm alone,'" she sang.

Grady closed his eyes as the words soaked into his soul. When the song was over he glanced at Chloe. She returned his look, a sidelong grazing of her eyes over his. But her smile lingered in his heart.

And he wondered if he dared let what he sensed was happening between them grow.

He held that thought and then Pastor Mathers came to the front of the church. He looked around, smiling as he welcomed the gathering, his blue eyes shining with friendliness. He made a few jokes, then asked everyone to bow their heads to pray.

His prayer was the usual invocation asking God to bless their worship time. To watch over them as they opened God's word. He also prayed that the past events of the community would not turn people against each other and that, instead, everyone would come together to help and support one another.

As the pastor prayed, Grady felt again the uneasiness that gripped him as he thought of the thefts that had been going on. It was making people testy.

Pastor Mathers finished his prayer and invited the congregation to turn to their Bibles. Grady followed along as the pastor read from *Isaiah* 40. He tried to listen but he was distracted by the beautiful woman beside him, her eyes on her Bible, a faint smile teasing her lips as if the words she read pleased her. He pulled his attention back to the pastor in time to hear him read, *"'Even youths grow tired and weary, and young men stumble and fall, but those who hope in the Lord will renew their strength. They will soar on wings like eagles, they will run and not grow weary, they will walk and not be faint.'"*

Pastor Mathers closed his Bible and looked over

the congregation, pausing as if to let the words settle into their collective mind. "In our culture and society these verses can be tough to swallow. We want to be strong. Independent. These are qualities we admire in ourselves and other people. But as Christians this is not how we are called to live."

Grady looked down, struggling with the pastor's words. It was as if the sermon were tailor-made for him.

You're a soldier, he told himself, mentally arguing with what the pastor said. *You have to be tough and strong. Weakness is death.*

But you're not a soldier anymore.

The other voice, the practical one he had spent the past few weeks ignoring, sifted back into his thoughts.

Didn't matter. He had to be strong. His brother was in the hospital. His grandmother needed him. Cody needed him.

He looked over at Chloe, who was looking at the pastor, her face holding a peculiarly skeptical expression.

As if she, too, struggled with the sermon.

Again he sensed she was keeping something to herself and again he wondered what.

In spite of his curiosity, he shook off the thought. He had enough going on in his own life. He didn't need to take on anything Chloe was dealing with.

* * *

"I miss you, buddy," Eva said to Cody, holding him close. The murmur of the people visiting after church rose up around the table they sat at in the hall attached to the church. Chloe felt a pang as she looked around the room. She recognized many of the people here, and as she and Eva chatted, a few members of the congregation stopped by to give her their greetings.

It was home and, for now, she was thankful for a job that kept her there.

"I think he misses you, too," Chloe said, reaching over to wipe some drool off his chin.

"Poor little motherless guy," Eva said. She looked over his head at Chloe, her expression curious. "I hear that Vanessa is gone. What do you think that means?"

That I don't have to put up with her condescending attitude.

Chloe simply shrugged. "I think she didn't like the fact that Grady was on to her lies."

Eva shook her head in dismay. "I sure hope we find out who he belongs to. Every baby needs a mother and father."

Chloe's heart skipped in her chest as she took Cody back from Eva. And what of her baby? She swallowed down a knot of panic, reminding herself of the song she had just sung. God was her refuge and fortress. He would guide her through the precarious place in her life.

"And Grady is most definitely not the father," Chloe said, settling Cody on her hip. He tried to grab for her necklace but she caught his hand, kissing his chubby fist.

"I'm sure that's a relief," Eva said with a coy smile.

Chloe pretended she didn't understand, unwilling to analyze her changing feelings for Grady. Sitting beside him in church had been more difficult than she had expected. She saw how earnestly he had listened to the pastor. How he had seemed to be pondering the message.

The same message that struck a chord with her. After she'd discovered that Jeremy hadn't returned to give their marriage another try as she'd believed, but had simply come to toy with her emotions, she'd promised herself she wouldn't let any man have any control over her again. She wouldn't let any man make her feel weak.

Yet now she was in a position of weakness, and though she didn't like it, she also knew it made her more dependent on God's guidance and provision.

All through the sermon she had kept wondering how Grady heard the message. Then she became frustrated that all her thoughts circled back to him.

"So, barring any other Stillwater coming out of the woodwork, I would guess that leaves Ben as Cody's father," Eva continued.

Chloe pulled her attention back to Eva and nodded. "It would seem that way."

"I just want to tell you how glad I am that you're helping at the ranch," Eva said, moving in closer as if she had some deep secret to impart. "Grady seems happier than when I saw him last."

Chloe frowned. "What do you mean?"

Eva gave her a mischievous smile. "I think you know what I mean. Though Grady has devoted himself to the army, he always said that one day he wanted to settle down at the ranch. Find himself the perfect girl and raise the perfect family."

The perfect girl.

That certainly wasn't her anymore.

Then across the room she saw Grady talking to Olivia Barlow, widowed mother of three children. Olivia brushed back her dark brown hair as she caught the hand of one of her triplet sons, frowning down at him as if warning him. She looked tired, and Chloe didn't blame her. The thought of raising her child on her own frightened her. She couldn't imagine doing it with triplets. Grady patted Olivia on the shoulder, as if in sympathy, then said something to the young boy. When Olivia left, Grady looked up, unerringly finding Chloe across the room. Their gazes locked.

Chloe's breath slowed and her heart raced. She pulled her eyes way only to find Eva watching her with a bemused expression.

"Someone just like you," Eva said with a self-satisfied smile. "I think you're exactly what my cousin needs."

Chloe's heart twisted at Eva's words. She knew she was starting to like Grady too much. She wished she knew what to do about it.

Chapter Six

"Smells wonderful in here." Mamie Stillwater stepped into the kitchen carrying a pile of dish towels that she had just washed and folded.

Chloe set the pan of freshly baked muffins on the counter, smiling at the results. "I thought I would bring some of these out to the hands. I'm sure they miss Martha Rose's cooking."

"I'm sure they do, though the boys can certainly manage without her until she gets back." Mamie set the towels in a cupboard beside the pantry and walked to the high chair Chloe had set close to the counter so she could watch Cody while she baked. "He looks tired."

Cody was rubbing his eyes, a piece of banana stuck to the back of his hand.

Chloe wet a cloth and quickly wiped him down. "He is. I just wanted to finish up here before I put him in bed. Sorry I didn't do it sooner."

Mamie waved off Chloe's excuses. "Honey, I wasn't trying to criticize you."

Chloe gave her a tight nod, realizing that her protest was automatic, hearkening back to her life with Jeremy. His constant criticism and harping had made her become overly aware of her shortcomings. It made her angry that he still had some influence on her behavior. She had promised herself she wouldn't be defined by his treatment of her.

Mostly she had kept that promise, but from time to time remnants of her old self returned.

"I can lay him down if you want," Mamie offered.

"No. I need these muffins to cool anyway." Chloe shucked her oven mitts and set them neatly aside, then pulled Cody out of his high chair.

A sudden and strong wave of nausea washed over her and she grabbed the edge of the counter to support herself. This was the worst she'd endured yet.

"Are you okay, child?" Mamie asked, suddenly concerned.

Chloe swallowed and swallowed, praying fiercely this would pass.

"Just feeling a little light-headed," she said as the vertigo receded. "I think I forgot to eat breakfast. And yes, I know breakfast is the most important meal of the day. My mom used to tell me that."

Mamie put the last towel in the cupboard and leaned back, her arms folded. "Do you remember much of your mother?"

"Bits and pieces. I was only ten when she died."

"That must have been hard for you and your father."

Chloe shifted Cody in her arms, tucking his warm head into the crook of her neck as her mind sifted back. "It was. My father was adrift without my mother. I think he barely remembered he had a daughter at times." She shook her head as if dislodging the memories, disliking the self-pity creeping into her voice.

"And then he remarried," Mamie said.

Chloe held Cody even closer as she recalled that moment when she'd realized Vanessa's mother did not see her as an asset, but rather as a rival for her father's affections. "That wasn't a good situation." She gave Mamie a wry smile. "Very Cinderella but with only one stepsister. And my dad didn't die. Etta left before that."

"Can I ask why she left?"

"A number of reasons," Chloe said, her voice growing hard. "She thought my grandfather would leave my father a boatload of cash, and when he died that was a disappointment. And then my father had his accident. He couldn't give her what she needed. Couldn't provide for her, and he had his injury, and what woman can live like that?" She gave Mamie an arch look, underlining the irony of her comment.

Mamie smiled sadly, clearly understanding what Chloe was saying and her slightly sarcastic inference.

"That can be hard," she said.

"I'll put this munchkin down and then I'll head out."

"I'm going to lie down," Mamie said. "I haven't been feeling well."

"I'm sorry to hear that," Chloe said, giving her a concerned look. "I can stay in the house if you want."

Mamie shook her head. "No. Cody will sleep. You go bring those boys some muffins. I'm sure they miss all the fussing they usually get from Martha Rose. I'll be fine."

Chloe nodded, then left with the little boy, but as she walked up the stairs she felt another wave of nausea and wondered how long she could keep her condition a secret.

And if it was fair to the Stillwaters to do so.

I just need this for a few more months, she promised herself. *Just until I can figure out what to do and where to go.*

The thought clung to her with icy fingers because at the moment she had no idea.

* * *

"That was a short break," Saul said, looking up from the horse he had just tied to a rail.

"Changed my mind," Grady said brusquely.

"Thought you said you needed a rest."

He had. His leg bothered him and while he resented resting it, part of him had been hoping to see Chloe. Until he'd overheard what she said.

...couldn't provide for her, and he had his injury, and what woman can live like that?

Though he didn't know the context of the words, it wasn't hard to infer what she meant, and it underlined his view of himself. Sure, he could take care of someone financially, manage the ranch from a desk like his father had, but that hadn't turned out well for his father, either.

A nasty wind with a bite to it swept through the alleyway, making Grady shiver. The forecast was for unseasonably cold weather. They would have to increase the cows' feed to compensate.

Josh Carpenter, one of the hired hands, led the horse Saul had just worked on back to the pasture. When he saw Grady, he stopped.

"Hey, boss, just wondering if I can take a day off this week?" he asked. "My dad needs my help setting up some surveillance cameras on his place."

"Has he been hit, too?" Josh's father wasn't

even a rancher. He lived on acreage on the edge of town.

"No. He's just getting paranoid that he might. Must have bought seven of those cameras. I tried to tell him that no one would want his old stuff, but to him it's precious."

"Should be okay." Emilio and Lucas would be around, so he could certainly spare Josh.

Josh gave him a goofy grin, which puzzled Grady until he realized the hired hand was looking at someone past him. He caught the same whiff of baking he had in the house and from the way his neck prickled he figured Chloe had just arrived.

"Hey, Chloe, good to see you," Josh said, threading his fingers through the reins of the horse he was still leading in a nervous gesture. He looked somewhat smitten and Grady couldn't blame him. Chloe seemed to have the same effect on him, except he tried a little harder than Josh to hide it.

"Good to see you, too," Chloe returned, stopping right beside Grady. In one hand she held a plastic bag, in the other a plate of muffins covered in wrap, their warmth creating a cloud of vapor on the covering. "I though you all might enjoy a snack."

"Just let me bring this cayuse away and I'll be right back," Josh said with a bright grin.

Though it had been only a couple of hours since breakfast, the smell of the baking made Grady's stomach growl. However, the thought of sitting all cozy and cute sharing some muffins with Chloe after what he had overheard was too difficult.

His mind scrambled to come up with a reason to leave, but then he made the mistake of looking at Chloe, who was smiling at him, her eyes bright and inviting, and he couldn't think of much at all.

"I could use a break," Saul said, lowering the horse's hoof and straightening. He patted the horse on the rump and walked over to join them. "I think we could set down right here." He hauled a couple of square bales together, making an impromptu sitting area. "You just set yourself down here, Chloe. Grady, you can drop down here." He grunted as he pulled over another bale. "And me and Josh can park ourselves right here."

Grady was now boxed in. Chloe to his right, the piled-up bales to his left and no escape.

He was fairly sure Saul had arranged that on purpose, so with a resigned sigh he sat down.

"So what kind of muffins are they?" Saul asked as he did the same.

"These are carrot pineapple," Chloe said, handing the muffins to Grady. "Can you unwrap them while I get some plates out for everyone?"

His stomach growled as he carefully took off

the plastic, memories assaulting him as he inhaled the scent. His mother in an apron while he and Ben ostensibly helped by cracking eggs, grating carrots but mostly making a nuisance of themselves, he was sure. The warmth of the kitchen, the giggles he and his brother had shared.

His heart hitched as he thought of the fight they'd had before Grady shipped out, his brother's anger at Grady's condemnation of his lifestyle.

"You okay?" Chloe asked, handing out the plates to Saul and Josh, who had quickly rejoined them.

He shook off the sorrowful memory, adding yet another prayer for his brother to come out of his coma. To give them another chance to be together.

"Yeah. I'm okay." He took a muffin and returned the plate for her to pass around. "These are my favorites."

"I got the idea from your grandmother," Chloe said as sat down beside him, the plate of muffins balanced on her lap. "She said you would appreciate them."

Grady took a bite and sighed. "These are as good as the ones my mom made." He took another bite, closing his eyes in bliss.

"You look happy," Chloe said.

He gave her a sidelong glance. "You sound as if that's important to you."

"It is, because I'm softening you up."

"Whoa, here comes the favors," Saul chortled, slapping his knee.

"What do you want?" Grady asked, feeling wary.

"To start physical therapy with you. Tonight. We already did the assessment, but you've been avoiding following through."

He stopped chewing, the muffin in his mouth suddenly tasting like sawdust.

"Besides, that's why your grandmother hired me," she continued, her hands folded primly on her lap, her head tilted to one side as if studying and analyzing him.

Her hair glistened in the light and the smile edging her soft lips resurrected a memory of her when they had been in school together. When he'd thought maybe there might be a chance for him.

He pushed that back, along with other dreams he'd had to discard along the way in his life.

"I don't need physical therapy," he said after swallowing the rest of the muffin. The last thing he wanted was Chloe seeing him more vulnerable than she already had.

"I know you do, and I know it will make a difference for you."

Grady quickly got to his feet. He didn't want to have this discussion, and he especially didn't want to have it in front of his hired hand and his farrier.

"I can take care of myself," he muttered, grabbing the crutch from the bale beside him.

Don't hurry, don't hurry, he told himself as he made his way down the alley of the horse barn.

The last thing he wanted, after that, was to fall down in front of Chloe.

And as he left her words seemed to taunt him. *He had his injury, and what woman can live like that?*

Chloe could only stare as Grady slid the heavy barn door closed behind him, effectively shutting her out.

Suddenly her little bribe seemed rather pathetic and ill thought-out. Had she really thought that waltzing in here with his favorite muffins would make this proud and stubborn man change his mind?

Josh jumped to his feet muttering something about the horses, leaving Chloe behind with a plate of still warm muffins and Saul's quiet company.

"Sorry about that," Saul said, reaching across the distance between them and covering her hand with his. "Grady hasn't been the same since he came back from Afghanistan. He would never admit it to me, let alone you, but I've known that guy since he was a kid. Always proud and self-sufficient. Always trying to be better than he was. I think he was always trying to make up for Ben's antics. Sometimes I think he took on too much. Joining the army was, I think, his way of bringing honor to the Stillwater name. It became a large part of who he is, and now he can't do that anymore." Saul leaned forward, stroking his handlebar moustache as he pursed his lips. "I think he sees himself as weak. For someone who has always tried so hard to be strong, this is a difficult thing. Especially with someone like you."

"What do you mean? Someone like me?"

Saul gave her a wry grin. "You haven't noticed how he acts around you?"

She didn't want to blush, thinking of that moment they had shared in the nursery.

"Doesn't matter," she said with a decisive note. "He needs to do the exercises or his muscles will pull his bones crooked, and we're looking at potential dysplasia and a host of other complications." She caught herself, realizing that Saul didn't need to know all that.

"I'm glad you're passionate about this," Saul said, patting her on the knee. "'Cause I think you will need every ounce of that persistence to get that man to agree. But just remember, he has a lot of pride. If you can find a way to work around that, you'll find a way to get him to agree. And if that doesn't work, just turn on your charm. I know that will be the ticket."

Chloe gave him a wan smile as she thought of the moments when their glances met and she'd felt an arc of awareness. But with that came a glimmer of sorrow. She wasn't the same innocent girl he had once cared for.

Chapter Seven

"I'm going to town today to see Ben," Grady announced after breakfast the next day. "Would you like to come along, Grandma?"

He thought if he kept himself busy today, he could stay out of Chloe's line of sight. Yesterday, when she corralled him in front of Saul and Josh, he had felt taken off guard. And that wasn't happening again.

Right now she was upstairs, busy with Cody. Even in the kitchen he could hear her singing as she bathed him, her voice as clear and true as it had been in church.

And as appealing.

His grandmother looked up from her breakfast and reluctantly shook her head. "I don't think I will. I didn't sleep well last night."

"Oh, no. I'm sorry to hear that," Grady said, rethinking his plans. He had counted on his grandmother driving him. He might have to get one of the guys to do it, though he hated to keep them from their work while he visited with Ben.

"Sorry I can't help you, but Chloe can come with you and take Cody along."

Grady frowned at that. "Why?"

"It would be good for Ben to spend time with his son," Mamie said, her voice firm, clearly misunderstanding his reluctance.

"You're right," he conceded. This would solve his transportation problem, but not the proximity problem. It was growing harder and harder to ignore Chloe. Harder and harder not to give in to the attraction he felt around her.

Well, it looked as if they would be spending the next few hours together. He slowly stood, stacking his bowl on his plate when his grandmother stopped him, as she always did.

"Here, let me take that."

"Grady can manage," Chloe spoke as she came into the room, Cody on one hip, her arms holding him close to her.

"But he has his crutch," Mamie protested.

"He can manage," Chloe said, her voice firm as she set Cody in the high chair and buckled him in.

Grady shot her a frown, wondering what she was up to.

"He doesn't seem to think he needs physical therapy, so I don't think he needs any help, either," Chloe said. "Clearly, he can take care of himself."

He grinned as she tossed his words of yesterday back at him. "I guess I can," he said. He held the plate, balancing it precariously as he limped over to the counter. He had to focus to make sure he didn't drop anything. No way was he making a fool of himself in front of Chloe.

"I'm leaving in a couple of minutes to visit Ben, but I'll need a ride," Grady said, turning to Chloe. "Would you be able to do that for me? And I was thinking we should take Cody, as well."

"If you can give me five minutes, I'll be at the front door."

He nodded, then worked his way down the hallway to his room, thankful it was out of sight of the dining nook. At the door to his room he took a moment to massage his leg. The past couple days the pain had been getting worse. He knew part of it had to do with all the walking around the ranch he'd been doing, checking on the cows, supervising the maintenance of the equipment that happened over the winter months, working with the girls in the Future Ranchers program.

Just do the therapy already.

Grady let the thought linger a moment, still not convinced it would make a difference.

But it won't hurt. And maybe you could go riding again.

Which was a consideration if his brother never came out of the coma.

He couldn't think that. Couldn't allow that to enter his thoughts.

But as he got ready to leave, it nagged at him.

"Has anyone told you about your brother's progress?" Dr. Searle, the neurologist, stood at the end of Ben's bed. He flipped through Ben's chart before glancing over at Grady and Chloe.

"No. We just got here," Grady said, looking from the doctor to his brother, who lay just as still as he had the first time Grady had visited. If there had been progress, he couldn't see it.

"We are seeing signs of Ben coming out of the coma," Dr. Searle said making a note on the chart and putting it back. "Last night he opened his eyes for a few seconds, then again this morning. That may not sound like much, but given how unresponsive he's been, it's significant."

"So do you know if he'll be...normal?" Grady hated to ask, but he needed to know.

"We have no idea of his mental or physical capacity as of this moment, but we are much more hopeful after the past twenty-four hours."

"So will he wake up if I talk to him?"

Dr. Searle simply shrugged. "We have no idea,

but I think you should talk to him as if he were conscious. Just act normal."

Grady looked down at Ben, feeling awkward. Talking to someone who didn't talk back still struck him as odd. "I feel kind of foolish doing that," he muttered.

"Just remember, it's not about you. It's about him," Dr. Searle said. Then he glanced at Chloe. "And how are you managing?"

"I'm working for the Stillwaters now," Chloe said, brushing a strand of Cody's hair away from his face.

"I was sorry to hear the hospital let you go. I hope you can eventually find something in your field."

Chloe just nodded, then looked back at Grady. "I'm thirsty. I'll go grab a coffee so you can talk to him alone."

Grady shot her a grateful look, thankful for her consideration. She gave him an encouraging smile and left with Dr. Searle. Grady dragged his attention back to his brother.

Ben looked pallid. The weeks spent in the hospital seemed to have shrunken him down. The tubes snaking in and out of him created a panic like an icy fist. What if his brother never fully regained consciousness? What if the angry words Grady had thrown at Ben just before he left were the last memory Grady would have of him?

"I'm sorry." He touched Ben's shoulder, then grasped it more tightly. "I'm sorry I said what I did. I know I sounded judgmental, but I said what I did because I cared...no, care about you," he corrected. "You're my brother, and I didn't want to see you throwing your life away. You've always been the only one who gets me, understands me, and I hope you get that I just wanted the best for you." He stopped there, feeling his throat thicken as he looked down at his brother, once so vital and alive, now seemingly inanimate.

He wondered if he should pray. Though he had enjoyed being in church, he still wasn't sure what to make of God's seemingly erratic answers to prayer. Had God truly been listening, He would have kept his fellow soldiers from being injured.

Would have kept him from being injured.

Yet as he stood by his brother's bed he felt two words rise up.

"Please, Lord" was all he whispered, and as he did, he gazed more intently at his brother, as if waiting for an answer.

But there was no change. No movement, just the steady beep of his heart monitor, the whirring of the IV machine. He could hear the muted chatter of the nurses beyond the ICU. The coming and goings of a hospital.

He should have known.

He stood a moment, looking intently at his

brother's eyelids, willing Ben to open his eyes, but when the silence grew more difficult than talking, he started telling Ben about the ranch, the program he'd begun and how well it was going. He brought him up-to-date on the goings on the thefts and the gifts, puzzling aloud why the Stillwater ranch hadn't been hit.

"Maybe it's because they feel sorry for you," he said with a light laugh. He chatted a bit more, slowly feeling less and less foolish.

Fifteen minutes later Chloe joined him, Cody still smiling and reaching out to him. "Ah, da, da, da," he burbled.

"Does he think I'm his dad?" Grady asked, suddenly alarmed.

"No. It's just a sound he makes. Apparently, that and *ah* are one of the first ones they make, so don't panic," Chloe said with a grin.

"Okay. Just to be clear. There's been enough confusion as to who this baby's father is," Grady said, relieved.

"I'm sure you're wondering who the mother is."

Grady looked back at Ben. In spite of his apology, Cody's presence only underlined the erratic and irresponsible life his brother had been living. "I wouldn't even have the vaguest idea," Grady said. "Ben had so many girlfriends and because I was gone so much I couldn't begin to keep up."

"In spite of being twins, you're very different," Chloe said.

"We weren't when we were younger. Dad always called us the Terrible Twos, and I think Mom's hair got grayer after we were born. But things shifted when we hit high school. I got more serious and Ben got wilder."

"I remember that," Chloe said, shifting Cody on her hip. "It got easier and easier to tell you two apart because Ben was the one always teasing me."

Grady just shook his head, not sure he wanted to know what Ben would be teasing Chloe about. "I just hope he knew when to quit."

"He quit when he got a rise out of me, so I learned to fake some anger or hurt or something so he could laugh and walk away."

"Was he mean?"

"No. Never mean." Chloe gave him a shy smile.

Grady held her gaze and his thoughts ticked back to that time. Ben used to tease him as well, telling him that sweet Chloe Miner had a huge crush on him. But she'd never indicated that she did. Then Vanessa had come on to him and they started dating. Which had only lasted a couple months—until graduation. Chloe had moved away after that and he never found out if it was true or not.

"I know he liked to exaggerate," Grady said.

"He seemed to have this idea that you had some kind of crush on me." He added a laugh, as if to show her that he didn't believe his brother.

To his surprise Chloe blushed.

Was it true?

"What can I say? I was young and impressionable and had a thing for cowboys." Chloe laughed it off, but Grady felt his own heart quicken at the thought.

He held her gaze, unable to look away, and before any second thoughts could assail him he said, "I wanted to believe my brother, but you never gave me any idea." His voice was quiet, sincere.

Chloe just stared at him, her blush deepening. But she didn't look away. "I was shy. And Vanessa told me that she liked you and that I better back off. I didn't think I stood any chance against her."

"You stood more than a chance," he said. He took a step toward her as if to close the distance between them. However, he didn't shift himself enough to raise his foot properly off the floor and he stumbled. She moved so quickly and caught him so easily, it was as if it hadn't even happened.

Except Grady knew it had and he couldn't stop the flush heating his cheeks.

He knew part of it had to do with the humiliation of almost falling in front of her, but he also knew it had as much to do with Chloe's proximity. The warmth of her arm around his back. The scent of apples that he guessed came from her shampoo. The warmth of her breath on his cheek. He shifted and their eyes met again and it seemed his resolve weakened again. He couldn't allow himself to be distracted by Chloe and her gorgeous green eyes. Her sweet and gentle nature.

He pulled away and moved closer to his brother, resting his hand on his arm, creating a connection between them.

"It must be hard for you," she said, moving Cody to her other arm. "Seeing your brother like this."

"Do you think he'll come out of it?"

"I wish I could tell you one way or the other. I'm not a doctor."

He just nodded, releasing a harsh laugh. "I was just talking to him like you suggested. Apologizing for what I said to him before I left for my last tour." He tightened his grip on Ben's arm as if hoping by force of will to wake him.

"What did you need to apologize for?"

Grady wasn't sure he wanted her to see him for who he really was, an irate and judgmental man who thought himself better than his brother, but he felt a need to tell someone. And who better than this gentle, caring woman?

"I got angry with him. I told him he was living a life unworthy of the Stillwater name. Told him that he didn't deserve to be a Stillwater. That he had to clean up his life." As he spoke, Grady heard again the harshness and condemnation he had thrown at his twin.

"What did he say to that?"

Grady caught his brother's limp hand, despairing over how lifeless it felt. How cool to the touch. As if Ben already had one foot in the grave and all it would take was one tiny push—

"He told me I didn't have any right to judge him. Told me that I was turning into a self-righteous jerk who thought he was better than anyone else." Grady stopped there, the pain of his brother's anger still so fresh.

"Was that the end of the argument?"

Grady nodded. "I walked away from him, got in my truck and left for my base. I shipped out the next day. We haven't talked since then."

Chloe was silent a moment. "That must be so difficult for you."

"I just wish I knew how to fix it." He gave her a sorrowful look. "When we were little we both had bad tempers. Whenever we fought, our parents would walk us through the reconciliation process. Now they're gone and I can't put this on my grandmother."

"I think you are taking too much on," she said. "The fact that Cody is here and clearly a Stillwater says something about the life your brother was living."

Grady felt an instant moment of defensiveness for his brother at her comment, but he relaxed. "I know. He hadn't embraced faith the way I had. My father's accident and my mother's leaving made him turn away from God. Which makes me feel even worse about our fight. The fact that it's unresolved. The fact that I should have been a better example of faith at work."

"You told him right? That you feel bad?"

Grady released a harsh laugh. "I did. For what it's worth."

"It's worth a lot. He knows now. And even if his brain can't sort it all out, I am pretty sure he can feel your love. As for his faith, that's in God's hands." She set Cody down beside Ben on the bed, close enough so he could touch Ben, but not so close that Cody could grab at the many tubes connected to him. "I'm hoping that by bringing Cody to see him, he builds an unconscious attachment to his son."

Grady looked from the baby to Ben and felt an unreasonable burst of jealousy. His brother, so irresponsible, had a son. A child.

Something he wanted for himself.

"This might sound a little strange to you, but how do you feel about praying with your brother?" Chloe said, shooting him a glance over her shoulder. "I know when you first came here you made a comment about leaving the praying to those who are more capable."

"It was a reactionary comment," he said, remembering that moment. "I still struggle with my faith, though. I've seen things that made me wonder about God."

Chloe reached over and touched his shoulder. A brief contact, but it was as if a current hummed between them. He knew he couldn't deny his attraction to her, though he still felt he couldn't act on it.

Her casual words from the other day still hung fresh in his mind.

"I'm sure we'll never understand what you've had to deal with, and this may sound like a cliché, but I know that God understands. I think we forget that He also carries the burdens of the world."

Grady shot her a wry glance. "You're smart for a young whippersnapper."

"I'm only two years younger than you."

"That's all?"

"It seemed like a lot in high school. At this point, it's minuscule." She shrugged. "And I've had my own difficulties." She said those last words quietly, as if to herself.

"Are you talking about your father?"

She blinked, as if she hadn't understood what

he'd said, then she nodded quickly. "Yes. Of course. Yes, I was talking about my father."

But as she looked away from him he caught a flare of anger in her eyes, a set to her jaw that was so completely out of character it jarred him.

He sensed she spoke of something else when she said that she'd had her own difficulties.

He wanted to ask her more, but she picked up Cody, walked around the other side of the bed and took Ben's other hand in hers.

"Did you want to pray with your brother?" she asked, avoiding his gaze.

Maybe God listened to her, he reasoned.

"I guess it can't hurt," he said, taking Ben's other hand, the unconscious man between them their only bond.

But just before he lowered his head he looked at her again and this time caught a look of utter sorrow in her eyes.

Chloe, it seemed, had her own secret sorrows.

And he wanted to know what they were.

Chapter Eight

"So have you discovered anything I can use?" Lucy rested her elbows on the table at Maggie's and released a heavy sigh, rubbing her forehead with her fingertips.

Though she had been in town yesterday, Chloe had asked for this morning off. Her father's lawyer wanted to meet with her to sign off the last of the papers for the estate. Lucy wanted to meet with her and Chloe had agreed, feeling as if she needed a break from Grady. He was growing far too appealing and his actions toward her were so confusing.

"Maddy Coles, the girl who got some gifts from the anonymous donors?" she said. "She works at the ranch through a program that Ben started."

"Really? Since when?"

"Since before I started there."

"Do you think it was before the thefts started?"

"I can find out."

Lucy stroked her chin as if thinking. "Maybe Maddy is the reason the Stillwater ranch hasn't had any thefts."

"Maddy was carrying around her iPod, but she didn't know who it was from. I didn't have a chance to talk to her any more than that."

"It's a start." Lucy sighed and pulled her hands over her face. "I just wish I could get one solid lead."

From the little bit of buzz Chloe had heard, people were growing increasingly weary of the thefts and the lack of action on the part of both Lucy's office and the Lone Star Cowboy League, which also was supposedly looking into the burglaries.

"But enough about me," Lucy said, an edge of determination in her voice. "How is your work at the ranch going?"

"I'm good. Cody is a sweetie and easy to work with."

"A far cry from Grady, I'd imagine," Lucy said with a wink. "Have you talked him into doing his exercises?"

"A work in progress," Chloe said taking a sip from her mug of tea. "I live in hope."

"You always did where Grady was concerned," Lucy goaded, picking up her coffee. "And now you're blushing even harder. Don't tell me you're falling for him again?"

Chloe knew that if she gave Lucy even the vaguest hint of what she felt for Grady, Lucy would drag every emotion, every nuance of every conversation between her and Grady out of Chloe. But she also knew Lucy wouldn't quit pushing until Chloe threw her even the tiniest crumb.

"It's…complicated," she said.

"What's complicated? You like him. You work there. You let him know. You're a beautiful girl, and you've got a lot to offer someone like him. Don't sell yourself short, my dear," Lucy said.

"Ever the matchmaker, aren't you?" Chloe said.

Lucy shrugged. "May as well try to get other people together. Guys usually don't go for the tomboy type like me."

"Now you're the one selling yourself short. You're a beautiful woman." *And you don't come with as many complications as I do*, Chloe thought as she tried to pull in her stomach. It was getting harder to hide her pregnancy. She knew sooner or later it would have to come out.

Lucy waved off her compliment. "I know who I am, and right now I've got more than enough to keep me busy. No time for romance."

"At least you have a job," Chloe said in a moment of self-pity.

"You've got a job now," Lucy said.

Chloe nodded. "I do and, don't get me wrong, I'm thankful for it, but I want to focus on physical therapy work. That's what I'm trained for."

"So what would be your dream job?" Lucy asked.

"What I'd like to do is open my own physical therapy clinic. With proper equipment and consistent care. The hospital does okay, but the program is not a priority there. I often think that if my dad had gotten better care and follow up he might not have ended up where he was."

"Can you use the money from your dad's estate to start it up?"

"I just met with dad's lawyer to finalize the estate, and it's official. There's nothing left. I won't be starting a clinic here or anywhere anytime soon." She blew out a sigh as she glanced around the bustling café and coffee shop, recognizing many of the people. When she had first moved back to Little Horn, she had nurtured some hope that somehow she would be able to stay here. This was home to her, and with a baby on the way, she wanted to be in a place where people knew her and she knew they would support her.

Fort Worth had been a cold, lonely place for her, but the way things were going, she knew she would have to move back there or some other large urban center where she could get steady work in her field.

Lucy touched her hand in sympathy. "That's too bad. I know you were hoping that could happen when you first moved here."

"It was a dream and I guess it will stay that." Chloe gave her a smile, then glanced at her watch. "I should get going. I promised Mamie I wouldn't stay long."

"I should, too." Lucy drank the last of her coffee and pulled her jacket off the back of the chair. "So you'll let me know the second you find anything out about Maddy or hear even the tiniest bit of gossip you think I might be interested in?"

"I will."

Lucy shrugged on her coat, adjusted it, her eyes still on Chloe, who was winding her own scarf around her neck. "And I still think you should give Grady a chance. I think you two would have ended up together if that snake of a stepsister of yours hadn't gotten in the way."

"If he really wanted to be with me—"

"I'm positive he would have, if you had let him know. Just like I'm sure something could happen between the two of you now if you just give him an idea of what you're feeling."

Chloe knew better, but her friend's encouraging smile ignited a spark of hope. She thought of that electric moment in the hospital yesterday when she had helped Grady after his stumble. When they had stood virtually face-to-face.

Could something truly happen?

She tried to dismiss the thoughts as she got up from her chair and pushed it back.

Lucy smiled at her and looked as if she was about to say something more when Byron McKay shoved past Chloe, almost knocking her over. He was a tall man, imposing, with a stomach protruding over the large, ornate silver buckle of his belt. His steely blue eyes seemed to impale her, as if it was her fault she had stumbled.

His teenage sons trailed behind him, hands in their pockets, their hoodies unzipped, shoulders hunched forward as if trying to make themselves invisible.

"Well, I'm sorry, missy," Byron said, his voice, as usual, carrying over the buzz of the café. He caught her arm to steady her. "Didn't see you there. You okay?"

Before Chloe could reply, Byron thankfully let her go and turned his attention back to Lucy. "So, Miss Sheriff, I don't imagine you've found out anything?"

"I would have reported it to the league if I did," Lucy retorted, her shoulders straightening, her chin up. "But now that I've got you here, I was wondering if you've heard anything from your cousin's daughter, Betsy McKay?"

"Why do you want to know about that crazy girl?" Byron said, his hands dropping on his hips in a defensive gesture, his voice growing belligerent. "Haven't heard a peep from her since cousin Mac died."

Chloe knew exactly why he was so prickly. Everyone in Little Horn knew Byron hadn't done anything for his cousin, Mac McKay, a struggling rancher who had ended up losing his ranch and, as a result, fighting a losing battle with alcohol. Mac had died about six months ago, and according to town gossip, Byron hadn't been bothered even to attend his funeral.

Mac's daughter, Betsy, had fled Little Horn in shame before she'd graduated high school. Hers was a sad story, but Chloe was curious why Lucy wanted to know about her.

"I was simply wondering how that poor girl is doing."

Byron snorted. "If she's anything like her loser father, she's probably getting into trouble." He laughed at his comment, looking over at his boys as if asking them to join in.

"That's a lousy thing to say, Dad," Gareth snapped, shoving his strawberry blonde hair back from his narrow face with an angry jab.

"You shouldn't talk that way about her father or her," Winston joined in, his hands now balled into fists at his sides. "She's our cousin."

"Can't think why you'd want to have anything to do with that washout family," Byron snorted.

Winston just shook his head, and both boys looked visibly upset with their father.

Gareth turned to Lucy. "We haven't heard from Betsy since she left Little Horn, but we're guessing she might be in Fort Worth."

"Probably living on the streets," Byron put in.

Winston's eyes narrowed and Chloe could not understand how the man could be so obtuse.

"Do you boys know Maddy Coles?" Chloe asked, thinking they might have heard some gossip through their other friends in high school as to why she ended up with the gifts she had. "She works at the Stillwater ranch."

"Other than that she was friends with Betsy, not much," Gareth suggested with a shrug. Winston simply shook his head.

"Stop this." Byron spun around, stabbing one long, thick forefinger at her, and Chloe felt a shiver of fear. "Why do you think my boys would hang around with some foster kid?" He glared at her and for a breath Chloe understood how this man could intimidate so many people.

But as he stared her down her back stiffened. Jeremy all over again.

And she wasn't allowing anyone to push her around again.

"Don't yell at me," she snapped, pushing his finger down and away from her.

Byron's eyes widened and Chloe felt suddenly sorry for the members of the cowboy league who had to put up with this man as their vice president, and for Carson Thorn who, as president, probably had to rein him in from time to time.

But to her surprise Byron didn't do anything more.

"Enough of this useless talk," Byron said, shooting one last glare at Chloe. "Boys, we're out of here."

He marched out of Maggie's, indignation trailing behind him like a cloud, and a sudden silence falling over the café.

Chloe pulled in a wavering breath, her knees suddenly weak after that confrontation.

"Wow, girl. I didn't think you had it in you," Lucy said, admiration tingeing her voice.

I didn't, either, Chloe thought, pulling in another breath. "I don't like pompous men yelling at me" was all she said.

"I'm officially impressed," Lucy said, zipping up her coat. "And glad you thought to ask about Maddy. I can't help think there's some connection between Maddy's gifts and the fact that the Stillwater ranch still hasn't been burglarized. Maybe Grady has some idea?"

They stepped out of the café just as an icy gust

of wind caught them. Lucy shivered, pushed her hands deep into her pockets and nudged Chloe with her elbow. "Hey, maybe you can get closer to Grady," she said with a mischievous grin. "You could be my honey trap. Use your charm and feminine wiles to get what you can out of him."

"He's been back only a couple of weeks," Chloe protested. "He doesn't know anything."

Lucy sighed. "I was just trying to convince you to flirt with the guy a little."

"He's my boss. There will be no flirting," Chloe said.

"I think you need to live a little. Who knows where it might get you this time?"

Chloe let that thought register for a moment, but then, right then, she felt a movement low down in her abdomen.

She stopped, eyes wide, her hand flying to her stomach as if to verify.

"What's the matter?" Lucy asked, stopping to see what was wrong.

Chloe's heart began racing. This was the first time she had felt the baby move. She felt it again, stronger this time. And in that moment the pregnancy that had felt so vague was now very real with all its consequences.

"Are you okay?"

Chloe just nodded and gave Lucy what she hoped was a reassuring smile. "I'm fine."

But as she walked out the door of the café and down the street to her car, she knew it would be a while before she would truly feel fine again.

Was that rain?

Grady rolled over in his bed, shedding the sleep clinging to him as what sounded like icy fingers tapped on the panes of glass. Frowning, he stumbled out of bed and looked out the window. Through the lines of frozen moisture on the glass he saw the blurry glow of the yard light.

Snow and sleet poured down, creating a sheen on the snow that had fallen overnight, and Grady groaned.

The forecast had been for a few scattered showers, which would have created its own difficulties. But this?

Freezing rain mixed with snow was a disaster in the making. He would have to wait until the sun was fully up before he knew just how bad things were.

He flicked on the light beside his bed. At least the power was still going, but if this sleet and snow continued, it could coat the lines enough that they would possibly snap.

He got dressed, more slowly even than yesterday morning, his leg even more uncooperative.

He rubbed the cramp in his thigh and breathed through the pain as he worked his pants up over his feet. Despair clung to him as another muscle spasm seized him and he wondered if this would ever ease off, but finally he was dressed. He grabbed the crutch, leaning on it even more heavily than before.

The thought of a cup of coffee lured him to the kitchen, as did a few moments of quiet before Chloe woke up.

It was growing increasingly hard both to avoid Chloe and to stop thinking about her. Thankfully she'd been gone yesterday morning so he could rest in the house for a while without worrying that she would give him that sassy little smile of hers that showed him she wasn't quitting.

The smile that made him far too aware of her appeal.

He knew he'd have to get past his changing feelings for Chloe. He kept hoping that time would ease them back into the past where they belonged, but every time he saw her they seemed to get worse. Trouble was he didn't know how long she would have to stay at the ranch taking care of Cody.

As for his own therapy, he knew he would have to give in sometime, but he also knew he couldn't work with Chloe. Maybe he could see someone in Fort Worth.

A long drive, which meant more time away from the ranch that he could ill afford.

He popped a pod into the single-serve coffee-maker, feeling the weight of his responsibilities. Then he heard a muted squall from upstairs. Cody was awake, which meant Chloe would be coming down soon, her green eyes probing as if waiting for him to give in.

He went to take out another mug for Chloe, but as he reached up into the cupboard another shard of pain shot through his leg and up into his back. He clenched his teeth, riding it out.

"Are you okay?"

Grady jumped, almost dropping the mug. He drew in a long, slow breath, leaning on the counter with one hand, and thankfully the pain subsided as it usually did. "Yeah, I'm fine," he said, flashing her what he hoped was an assuring grin.

She wore an old plaid shirt hanging loose over a pair of jeans so faded they looked gray. One knee was ripped and the hems were ragged. Her feet were bare, her hair still tousled, though she had made an attempt to tame it by pulling it back. A faint line of mascara still smudged her eyes.

Yet she still managed to make his heart beat faster.

She stared at him with what he thought of as her professional look. As though he was some specimen she was examining. But to his surprise she said nothing about therapy or exercises, even

though he was obviously leaning on the counter
to take weight off his injured leg.

"I thought I heard Cody," he said, setting one
mug on the coffeemaker and pressing the button.

"He's fussing a bit, but not fully awake. Kind
of like me," Chloe joked, walking past him to
pull the creamer out of the refrigerator. She set it
on the counter, then took a couple of spoons out
of one drawer and put them by the coffeemaker.
"Sounds as if it's blowing hard out there," she
said, stifling a yawn.

"It looks quite nasty. Snow mixed with sleet.
I'm wondering what the roads will be like."

The lights flickered and both of them looked
up at the ceiling as if waiting for them to extin-
guish.

Chloe pushed away from the counter, walked
to the bay window and shoved aside the heavy
curtains. "Doesn't look good," she said. "I don't
think anyone will be going anywhere in this."

"I guess I'll have to make some calls," Grady
said, getting another cup ready. "No sense having our hands risking an accident just to get to
work today."

"Can you manage without the hands around?"

Grady shrugged, the gnawing pain in his leg a
reminder of the extra work he had done yesterday
with Emilio and Josh as they'd fed the cows that
were close to the ranch. "Cows will be good for a

couple of days. I'll have to get Emilio to feed the cattle at the other place. He's got a tractor there at his disposal, so they should be okay."

They would have to get a few of the horses in, however. Two more besides Sweetpea were in foal, and he didn't want to risk them falling on the ice and losing their babies. He would have to figure out how to do that; the thought of navigating the ice with a crutch gave him the willies.

"You should call Maddy and the other girls and let them know, as well."

"I doubt their parents would let them come anyway," Grady said, stirring in some sugar and cream into the coffee and setting her cup on the eating bar by the counter. "Your coffee is ready."

She came back to the kitchen and was about to pick up the creamer when he stopped her.

"I already did that."

She pulled her head back in surprise. "Really?"

"Yeah. One sugar and about a quarter cup of cream."

"Not that much," she protested.

"Pretty close," he teased.

She settled on a stool across from him, cupping her hands around her mug, and gave him another smile. "Thanks so much. I'm surprised you remembered."

"All part of my training to observe."

She took a sip of her coffee and released a sigh

of pleasure. "That's just perfect." She rested her elbows on the eating bar, her coffee cup cradled between her hands as she watched him. "You've been in the army since graduating high school, haven't you?"

Grady nodded, stirring some cream into his own coffee. Most of his life he drank it black but that was more convenience than anything. Cream was a luxury he never indulged in except when he was stateside. "I've been in special ops for the past three years."

"Green Beret, I understand," Chloe said, her voice full of admiration.

Grady felt a dull ache in his chest. "Not anymore."

Chloe nodded as if acknowledging his loss.

"Though it's just as well right now with Ben in the hospital," he said before she could jump in with some platitudes about how if he did the work he could be back at his old job in no time. The same facts his army doctor had thrown at him. The facts immediately negated by the physical therapist he had worked with in the hospital. "I've got enough happening in my life anyhow."

"When Ben comes out of his coma, would you go back? To the army?"

Grady thought of the training position his superior had offered him as he took a sip of his own coffee, one hip leaning against the counter for support. It didn't hold any appeal. "I can't go back to doing something less than before." Then he gave her a melancholy look. "But I like you how said *when*, not *if* when you talked about my brother. As though it's a foregone conclusion that Ben will come back to us."

"I'm not the kind of person to throw out things just to make people feel good. The last time we visited Ben the doctor said Ben was showing signs of wakefulness. I feel fairly positive."

"You always were a positive person," he said.

"Not always so positive. There were times..." She let the sentence slip away unfinished.

"What times?" he prompted, curious as to which part of her life she referred to, wondering if it was connected to the sorrow he saw in her eyes that afternoon in the hospital.

She pulled in a deep breath, her face holding a puzzling hurt, then she shrugged as if shucking off whatever memories clung to her. "Doesn't matter."

But suddenly it did. To him.

Cody started wailing in earnest, Chloe took a gulp of her coffee and without another look his way slipped off the stool and hurried upstairs. Grady watched her, yearning to find out what she was talking about.

Then the phone rang.

Grady answered. Josh was on the other end

telling him that he couldn't come to the ranch. He was stuck in his yard.

After Grady hung up he walked over to the window. Though the day was dawning, it was still dark and gray outside, but there was enough light to show him ice and snow clinging with a treacherous grip to fences, buildings and roads.

No one would be coming and no one would be leaving.

Until the storm let up and the weather got substantially warmer, Mamie, Cody, Chloe and Grady were stranded.

Chapter Nine

"Where are you going?" Chloe asked as she came down the stairs.

Grady wore his heavy winter coat and was limping toward the porch.

"Is Cody asleep?" he asked, not answering her question.

"Down for his morning nap."

"How's my grandmother?"

"She's reading in her bed."

This morning after she had fed Cody his breakfast, Chloe had gone to check in on Mamie Stillwater, who hadn't gotten up at her usual hour. The dear woman had said she was too tired to get up, so Chloe had brought her some tea and toast, both of which had been gone when Chloe got back.

"Do you think we'll need to take her to the doctor?"

"No. I think it's just a cold," Chloe said, carrying what was left of the bottle she had given Cody to the sink. "She doesn't have a fever and thankfully she's not coughing." She emptied the bottle's contents and rinsed it out, then put it in the dishwasher.

Chloe suspected his grandmother was simply tired and run down. The past few months had been stressful for poor Mamie. It was no surprise she might be coming down with something.

"I better get going," Grady said.

"Where?" Chloe had checked the weather on the computer in the office and it talked of school and road closures and travel advisories. Though it was still storming, she could tell the yard was also impassable.

"I have to bring the horses into the barns."

"Surely you're not doing that now? By yourself?"

"I have to. Two of them besides Sweetpea are in foal and need to come inside."

Chloe couldn't stop her glance down at his leg and the crutch he was picking up. She wanted to protest but then thought of what Saul had told her about Grady feeling less like a man as a result of his injury.

"I can help you," she said. "Cody and your grandmother are both in bed and won't need me for at least an hour."

"I'll be okay," Grady said.

"Of course you will, but it wouldn't hurt to have an extra set of hands around horses in a storm."

Grady gave her an oblique look, as if he wasn't sure of her motives but then, to her surprise, he gave her a tight nod. "Okay. Just make sure you don't fall on the ice."

Chloe clamped down an automatic response. "I'll let your grandmother know what's happening and I'll get my cell phone in case she needs to get hold of us."

But by the time she came back down, Grady was already outside.

"Stubborn man," Chloe muttered, yanking on her coat, tugging a stocking cap down over her ears and pulling her gloves out of her pockets. She got her winter boots on quick enough and stepped out the door. Her feet slid out as soon as she set foot on the sidewalk. Flailing her arms, she regained a precarious balance on the slick ice and snow, and moved more slowly across the yard as the sleet beat at her with icy needles. If she squinted she could just make out Grady's dark shape ahead of her, his crutch far out to the side, giving him support.

She caught up to him just as he got to the barn and before he could protest, which she knew he would, she reached past him and pulled hard on the handle. The door, probably frozen on its rails, didn't budge. She tried again, bracing herself. This time Grady helped her and together they manhandled the door open.

Inside, the barn was a haven of darkness and quiet. The storm, muted by the heavy wooden walls, sounded less menacing in here.

Chloe brushed some snow off her hair and turned to Grady, who was closing the barn door. He flicked a switch and golden light bathed the cool interior.

"So where are the horses?" Chloe asked, shivering as a piece of snow melted down her neck. Sweetpea nickered at them, as if telling them they needed to get the other ones inside.

"Out in the pasture off the training pens," Grady said. "We'll need to get most of them into the corrals first before we can sort out which ones we want in the barn."

Though Chloe had worked with the horses on her father's ranch, she also knew that she would have to be cautious working with someone else's animals. She didn't know their pecking order or their behaviors. She would have to be careful and, at the same time, watch Grady. She took a quick breath, sent up a prayer and then followed Grady to the tack room.

"We'll hang these just inside the door. I don't want the horses seeing them until we've got most of them penned up."

"Good idea," she agreed.

She walked alongside him, trying not to ignore his hurried but awkward movements. The last thing she wanted was another accident, she thought, her palms growing damp inside her gloves.

"Ready?" Grady asked as they arrived at the far door of the horse barn leading to the horse corrals. He gave her a conspiratorial grin and she felt herself relax. Grady had faced far worse than this, she reminded herself. He had been born and raised around horses and knew them.

Chloe tugged her hat down on her head, then nodded. As soon as they stepped outside, the wind sucked her breath away and ice stabbed her face. She kept her focus on Grady ahead of her. In the distance she heard the whinnying of horses as Grady opened the fence to the pasture. The sun was coming up, turning the pitch black into a dark gray. As she squinted through the blinding snow, a vague outline of dark shapes ran toward them, growing clearer with each step.

"Here they come already," Grady shouted. "Open the gate to the corrals. Ten feet ahead of you to your right."

Slipping and sliding over the icy snow and clinging to the fence for support, Chloe made her way to the gate. With chilled hands she fumbled with the latch of the chain holding the gate closed. Finally she got it undone, the howling wind unable to mask the growing thunder of the horse's hooves. She pushed on the metal gate with its frozen hinges, stifling her own panic.

She heard Grady shout, the momentum of the horses slow and as she got the gate open, they swept past her, throwing up snow and ice, panting as they ran into the corral.

"The ones I want are in that bunch," Grady called out. "Close the gate. Close the gate."

The horses, now milling in the corral, seemed to sense they were hemmed in and were already turning to come back out when Chloe pushed the gate shut, her feet skidding on the slick ice. The gate clanged shut and the lead horses stopped, slipping and sliding, but, surprisingly, keeping their footing.

"You're better on ice than I am," Chloe grumbled, her hands frozen as she wrapped the chain around the fence post and the corral gate. Her gloves were stiff and her fingers unresponsive, but she finally clipped the chain closed.

She leaned against the gate, shivering as she breathed out a heavy sigh of relief.

Grady came up beside her and clapped a hand on her shoulder. "Great job. Thanks. I couldn't have gotten them in myself."

She nodded, realizing that only part of their work was done. The pen was icy and the horses, most likely riled up by the storm, tossed their heads around, snorting and restless. She didn't look forward to going in there.

"Which ones do you want?" she asked, hunching her shoulders against the biting cold.

"Babe and Shiloh. The roan mare with the blaze and the appy." Grady blew out his breath, as if also anticipating the difficulties they would face.

"I'll get the halters."

When she got back, Grady was already in the pen, oblivious to the ice pelting him, his hand out, calming down the horses. She was surprised at how much they had settled already, but she knew catching the pregnant mares and getting them separated from the herd would still be dicey.

She climbed the fence, slowly and deliberately just as her father had taught her, her pants sticking to her legs, her thighs and hands numb with cold.

Keeping the halter behind her back, she walked toward Grady, who stood in front of the group of horses, holding his hand out to calm them down.

"Do you dare go to Shiloh, the appy, and get her?" Grady said, raising his voice just loud enough for her to hear. "I'll get Babe."

Chloe bit her lip in apprehension, but she nodded as she handed Grady the halter. She moved toward the horse, wishing she could have come up beside her rather than head-on, a gesture horses often interpreted as a threat. As Chloe approached, Shiloh tossed her head, as if establishing her independence but, to Chloe's surprise, didn't move. Chloe wrapped her arm around the horse's neck, grabbing the halter rope and slipping it around. Then she got the halter on, fumbling with the buckle with unresponsive fingers. One down, she thought, tugging on the halter rope when the horse didn't want to move.

Chloe brought Shiloh to the fence and tied her up, then went to see if she could help Grady.

He had managed to get the rope around Babe's neck, but she tossed her head, resisting. Grady clung to the rope with one hand, to his crutch with the other as he wavered on his feet. Babe pulled back, Grady's crutch slipped on the ice and he spun around.

With a pained cry he barely kept his balance, but the rope fell out of his hand, the halter fell to the ground and Babe, with another toss of her head, ran around Grady, the other horses following.

For a panicky moment all Chloe saw was milling horses and through their legs, Grady, trying to find his crutch.

Chloe waved the horses away, yelling at them. Thankfully they trotted to the other side of the corral, and Chloe hurried to Grady's side.

"Are you okay?" she asked, grabbing him by the shoulders, her panicked gaze flicking over him.

"I'm okay," he grunted, fitting his crutch, now coated with snow and dirt, under his arm, staggering. "I'm fine."

But she could see by the way he pressed his lips together and his narrowed eyes that he wasn't. She helped steady him, grabbing on to his coat with her frozen hands.

They stood, their eyes locked, their breaths mingling. Chloe felt her heart quicken as Grady reached up and touched her face with one gloved hand.

"Chloe," he said, that one word encapsulating everything building between them.

Then another gust of wind pelted her with snow, bringing back reality with an icy slap.

"Stay here. I'll get Babe," she said.

Grady protested but she ignored him. She grabbed the halter rope from the ground, hunched her shoulders against the bone-chilling cold and with cautious steps walked toward Babe. Chloe knew enough about horses that the mare would be harder to catch the second time around, but Chloe was cold and miserable herself, her emotions riding a mixture of anger and fear at Grady's near miss and in no mood to be trifled with.

"Come here, you nutty creature," she said, her

low-pitched, singsong voice masking her anger. "Time to find out who is boss."

Babe watched her approach as if debating what to do. Chloe took advantage of the horse's hesitation, moved directly toward her and with quick, sure movements got the rope around the horse's neck. She gripped it tightly with one hand while she flexed the frozen fingers of her other hand and slipped the halter on. Her gloves made handling the buckle awkward so she tugged them off with her teeth. The cold buckle stuck to her fingers, but she disregarded the pain as she forced the unyielding strap through.

Done. She grabbed her gloves and brought the horse back, hoping she would be able to untie Shiloh with her numb hands.

"I'll take her," Grady said, but Chloe ignored him, pulled on the bowline knot she had tied on Shiloh's halter rope. Thankfully the icy rope pulled free and without a backward glance at Grady, she brought both horses to the gate. She unlatched it and got the horses through. A quick look showed that Grady was close behind her, latching the gate.

The barn door slid open on its rollers and she quickly led the horses inside, shivering with reaction at the cold penetrating every square inch of her.

The barn was warm in comparison to the storm

raging outside. Sweetpea put her head over the gate, whinnying as if welcoming the newcomers. Chloe put Shiloh in the first open stall she found, shut the door with one hip and then put Babe in the one next to her. By the time Grady was back in the barn, she had the halters off and was shutting the door on Babe's pen again.

She stood, halters hanging on the ground, her hands like two blocks of ice, glaring at Grady as he turned to her.

"You scared the living daylights out of me," she said, her voice controlled, masking a fury that gripped her in an icy fist.

"Sorry. It was an accident." He yanked off his hat, slapping it on his thigh to dislodge the snow.

"Caused by your stupid pride and your disability."

Grady's head whipped up at that and his eyes narrowed. "What are you saying?"

"I'm saying that this is enough," she said, shaking the halters at him. "You have held out long enough. Yeah, I get that you're tough and independent and too manly to accept help, but you could have been killed out there. If you were by yourself, you might have."

"I've faced death before," he returned, his voice growing harsh, cold. "I'm not afraid to die."

"Very brave and very noble. But you've got people depending on you, so you don't have that choice anymore. Ben needs you, Cody needs you and your grandmother needs you. Those kids that your brother has started that program for need you." She stopped before she could add "I need you." It was there, hovering, like a live thing but she knew she could never voice that thought. She had no right to need him.

She pulled in a breath, calming her anger, her hands now resting on her hips in a gesture of defiance and challenge. "Tomorrow you and I are starting your physical therapy. You have no place to go and neither do I until the roads are cleared, so get ready 'cause it's happening."

Then, to her surprise, he sank down on a bale by the door and shook his head. "You're right. I need to do this."

She was momentarily taken aback. She had already been marshaling her arguments, ready to beat down any protests he might make, but clearly they weren't necessary.

"Okay. Tomorrow morning in the exercise room downstairs. Right after Cody's breakfast." She'd had the room ready since she had come. Now she could finally use it.

"Sure. I know I've been fighting it, but…whatever." He shoved his hand through his hair in a gesture of defeat.

"I'll need you to work hard. *Whatever* isn't enough get you through this."

He looked up at her, then gave her a crooked smile that didn't help her own equilibrium. "I'm sure you'll put me through my paces. I saw you with Babe. I don't think I'd want to cross you."

"Darn tooting," she said.

"You were amazing out there," he said, his smile softening. "I'm suitably impressed. You have a way with horses."

"I grew up on a ranch, too," she said, feeling a bit too breathless as an unwelcome perplexity gripped her. She felt as if the world turned in quiet, increasingly smaller circles, with them at the center. Nothing else existed in this moment. She cleared her throat, trying to chase away her confusion. "I was always more of a tomboy than my stepsister."

"Vanessa has nothing on you, Chloe Miner. And don't let yourself fall into that way of thinking. You're twenty times the woman she is and many others besides."

Chloe swallowed, his praise creating a flush that chased away the chill that had stung her cheeks only moments ago.

"Let's get these horses some feed and then we can go," she muttered, feeling as if the breath had been sucked out of her chest.

Stay focused, she reminded herself. *You'll be spending a lot of time with him. Keep yourself aloof.*

But as they dumped hay in the stalls, she ignored

the sensible voice and chanced a sidelong glance only to see him looking at her. And for a moment, neither looked away.

"This silly exercise can't be doing anything," Grady grumbled as he pushed his thigh over what Chloe called a foam roller. "This isn't even my injured leg and it hurts."

Chloe had set up some mats downstairs by the exercise equipment Ben had set up at one time. "To make myself buff for the ladies," he had told Grady when he had asked him about it.

Now it sat there, unusable by both Ben and Grady.

"Pain is just weakness leaving the body," Chloe joked, kneeling beside him, supervising. "But as for not doing anything, this silly exercise helps loosen the muscles of your outer thigh. Because you tend to favor your injured leg, your other muscles overcompensate and slowly go out of whack."

Grady stifled a groan as needles of pain stabbed his thigh. "Whack. Is that a technical term?" he ground out.

"It's Greek for messed up."

Grady couldn't help a responding laugh, which was stifled by another jolt of pain. He had done some physical therapy when he was flown back to the States, but he had cut the program short when he'd found out about his brother. So he had left, promising to follow up.

He certainly hadn't thought the follow-up would involve working with Chloe.

Outside the storm still blew, creating havoc for anyone wanting to drive. Thankfully the mares were safely in the barn. The rest could fend for themselves.

Cody was sleeping and his grandmother, who had been quite tired the past couple of days, said she would take care of him.

At this moment it was just him and Chloe. If it wasn't for the fact that she had her professional face on, he wondered if something else wouldn't be happening.

"Do you think my grandmother is okay? Should we phone someone?" he asked, grunting as he did a few more passes over the roller, trying to distract himself from Chloe's presence. "Do you think we should call a doctor?"

"I think she's just tired," Chloe said. "I'm no doctor, but from what I can see she's healthy, eating well. Just feeling a bit peaked. It's just as well we're stranded for a few days. It will give her some chance to catch her breath and get some rest."

"You're a woman of many talents, you know," he said, flashing her a smile.

To his surprise she blushed. He knew he hadn't

imagined the uptick in his own heart rate at the sight. Precisely the thing he had been concerned about when he'd discovered Chloe would be working with him, was happening. His feelings for her were growing with every moment they spent together.

He returned his attention to his exercises, promising himself he would stay focused, and for the next few minutes as Chloe shifted the angle he was working, it was all he could do to work through the pain.

Finally he was done, and as he eased himself off the roller, he lay on his back looking up at the ceiling of the basement rec room, surprised at the sweat beading on his forehead. Though the exercises Chloe had set up for him seemed basic and unchallenging he found himself breathing hard now, heart pounding.

"Congratulations," Chloe said, handing him a towel and holding out a bottle of water as he sat up. "You've just completed your first round of physical therapy with me."

"First of how many?" Grady asked, taking a long drink of water.

"That will depend on your progress and how long your grandmother wants me around."

Grady set the bottle aside and wiped his face, trying not to think about the upcoming sessions. He'd had a hard time being objective around

Chloe when every time she had to show him how to position himself he'd been far too aware of her touch. Of the fresh scent of her hair.

She held out her hand to help him up, but he ignored it, struggling to his feet and walking over to the weight bench. Hard not to feel less of a man when you could barely stand on your own.

At one time he'd been the guy other men looked up to. He'd been the guy other guys wanted to be like. A Green Beret.

Now he was reduced to rolling his thigh on a foam roller, the most basic of exercises reducing his muscles to a quivering mass. At one time in his life he could run fifteen miles with a fully loaded backpack. Now a few leg lifts and stretches took everything out of him. He couldn't imagine trying to get on the back of a horse.

The thought gutted him and he pushed it aside. Another time. Another place. Right now he had other priorities.

"It gets better, you know," Chloe said as he regained his balance and sat down on his brother's weight bench. He needed to rest his tired muscles a moment. "And if it's any consolation, you aren't in as bad a shape as I thought."

"A minor consolation." He took another drink and slung the towel around his neck, watching Chloe gather up the equipment. "I know it's late, but thanks again for helping me with the horses yesterday. I couldn't have brought them in without you."

"I was glad to help," she said, her smile creating a current of awareness that he had a harder time ignoring each moment they spent together.

"I was glad to have your help, though it kills me to admit it."

"Why?"

He released a short laugh. "No man likes to admit he needs help."

"Especially not a Green Beret?" she teased as she set the roller aside. "Don't tell me that you did all your missions on your own. Solo. By yourself."

"No. Of course not."

"You were part of a team and each member had their own strengths. You depended on each other."

"Yeah. We were a team."

"I think that's what life is all about," she said, folding the towel he had just used and laying it in the laundry basket. "Helping each other. Leaning on each other."

He said nothing at that, trying to put what she said into his own life.

"I can tell you don't believe me," she continued.

He sighed, then turned to her, feeling that since she had seen many of his weaknesses the past few days, what did he have to lose by showing a few more?

"It's not that I don't believe you. It's just that it's hard for me to see myself as less than who I used to be."

"Why less?"

"I'm not the same man. I used to be able to do so much more. I feel as if I lost part of myself. Part of who I was proud of."

"Well, you know the old saying, 'Pride goeth before a fall.' And I'm sure you've had enough of those, as well."

In spite of himself, he laughed at her gentle teasing. "And will probably have more, so I guess I better get used to swallowing. My pride, that is."

Chloe laughed at that, as well.

"I have to ask, do you think I'll be able to ride a horse again?"

"Of course you will," she said. "Once you get your muscles working the way they're supposed to and you've got some more strength in your leg. No reason at all. In fact, riding will be good therapy for you. Your muscles are always working."

"So you rode a lot?"

"I loved riding."

"How many horses did your father have?" he asked.

"Only four. Mostly for pleasure riding. Dad

used an ATV to round up the cows. Not much of a cowboy purist."

"Plus his land is flatter, which made it easier to get around with one of those," he said. "So what is happening to your father's ranch?"

"It's sold now. Clark and Jane Cutter bought it."

"That's too bad. He didn't want to will it to you?"

"There was nothing left to will. Dad owed too many people too much money. Left a few hanging."

The short tone in her voice made him realize a few more things were going on that she seemed reluctant to share.

"I'm sorry. I didn't know." He watched her, suddenly remembering the exchange between her and the farrier.

"Saul knew your father, didn't he?"

Chloe nodded, folding up the last of the towels she had used. "He was an old friend of the family."

"What did he mean when he said that he was sorry? About the funeral?"

Chloe's hands slowed, her brow furrowed, and Grady guessed he had strayed into territory she didn't want to follow.

"I'm sorry," he said, tossing the empty bottle of water into a bin. "I shouldn't be so nosy."

"No. It's fine," she said, her voice quiet. "Saul and my father had a huge fight just before my father died. Knowing Saul, I'm fairly sure it was about my father's drinking."

Grady heard the shame in her voice and wanted to console her somehow. "That must have been hard for you. Not to have him come to the funeral."

"I don't blame Saul on the one hand. They had drifted apart long before that. Saul had warned my father not to marry Etta, but he did anyway. That was the beginning of the end of their friendship."

"Etta being Vanessa's mother."

Chloe turned away from him, nodding.

"That marriage must have been hard for you, too?"

"My father was so lonely after my mother died, and when he met Etta I think he figured she would fix that." Chloe picked up the empty water bottle he had set aside and put that in the basket as well, not looking at him, her expression pensive.

"So what happened between them that made her leave?"

"A few years after they got married, my grandfather passed away. And we got to find out how badly Gramps had managed the finances. My father didn't inherit as much as Etta seemed to think he would. Then my father had his accident with his ATV. She couldn't live poor and with a disabled man, so she left."

"So how long were Etta and Vanessa at the ranch?"

"About three years. Most of high school. I was excited when Vanessa first moved in," she continued. "I was looking forward to finally having a sister, but…"

She stopped herself there and Grady guessed what her next comment would be. "She wasn't the easiest person."

"I had so hoped to be close to her," Chloe said, grabbing a spray bottle and cleaning cloth. "But that never happened. I liked riding and being outside and she preferred makeup and magazines and boys. We were so completely different." She sprayed the mat he had just used and glanced up at him. "I guess you can't identify. You and your brother always seemed so close. I guess it was because you are twins."

"We used to be close," Grady said, rubbing his hand over his still-sore thigh. "Used to do everything together. But after high school, after Dad had his accident and my mother left, we drifted apart." He released a harsh laugh. "You'd think we would have become closer after that, but we didn't. I signed up for the army after my mother left. My way of coping…of making sense of life. Ben chose his own path."

"I'm sure losing your mother was a difficult time for you both."

"And you know what that's like, don't you?"

"You feel adrift."

Chloe sounded wistful and he felt sympathy flood his soul as their gazes met in an instant of shared grief. "But you found your way, didn't you? You became a physical therapist. You got married."

"I did," she said, turning away, wiping the mat and pushing herself to her feet.

"So how did you and your ex-husband meet?"

"Not my best moment. We met in a bar. He seemed nice." She grew quiet and he sensed an underlying disconnect.

"Seemed nice?"

She released a short laugh. "I was impression-able."

Which only made him more curious. He knew he had to stop. He was moving into places in her life he had no right to go.

So why did her terse replies only raise more questions he wanted the answers to?

He watched her, letting his feelings for her rise up, wondering if he dared act on them.

Then she looked over her shoulder at him and it was as if an electric current hummed between them.

He felt as though it wasn't a matter of *if* he would give in to the appeal she created, but *when*.

Chapter Ten

"You did good today," Chloe said to Grady as she poured a cup of coffee for him. "Your second day of therapy and I can see some progress. Couple more weeks of this and I'm sure you'll notice the difference."

Grady just groaned his response, his eyes closed, head resting on the back of the leather couch he had dropped into after supper. He had just come in from feeding the horses for the night.

The storm, now in its second day, still raged outside, still cut them off from everyone else. Chloe and Grady had gone out this morning to check on the horses and then, when they'd come back, Chloe had put him to work.

She had managed to get in another session this afternoon, but now they were done for the day.

A fire crackled in the fireplace of the living room, sending out blessed warmth. The lights had

been turned low, creating a cozy, intimate setting. Mamie sat on the couch across from Grady,
reading a book, a blanket wrapped around her
legs. For someone who was supposed to be ill
she looked quite perky, Chloe thought.

"The second day of therapy is always the hard-
est," she said. "Mamie, did you want more coffee?"

Mamie looked up from the book she was reading and pulled off her glasses. She released a
heavy sigh. "No. I'm still not feeling well. I think
I might turn in."

"I still think we should call a doctor," Grady
said, lifting his head to frown at his grandmother.

"I'm not that ill. I just need rest." She gave
Chloe a wan smile. "I'll check on Cody before
I go to bed. You two just stay here." She set her
book down on the small table beside the couch,
glasses neatly on top, set her blanket aside and
made a show of getting to her feet.

Chloe watched her little performance, and her
feeling that Mamie wasn't being entirely truthful
was borne out when she got a faint wink from
Mamie as she walked past.

Was she deliberately leaving the two of them
alone?

The thought made her flush again. She wasn't
sure what to do about her changing feelings for
Grady, and she knew being alone with him would

make it harder to keep herself aloof from him. In fact, the past few days her determination to stay focused on her job had been more difficult the more she got distracted by attraction she sensed growing between them.

She placed her hand on her stomach, as if to remind herself of the single reason she had to keep her heart whole. The secret she knew she couldn't keep quiet much longer. Sooner or later she had to tell Mamie at least. But it was her innate sense of self-protection that made her keep her secret. Thankfully she could wear looser clothing today while she worked with Grady so she could demonstrate some of the exercises she wanted him to do. But her clothes were getting tighter. She was getting close to five months now. She knew she would start showing soon.

"I should get to bed, too, but I'm too lazy," Grady said, easing out a sigh as he reached for his coffee. "I figure I've done enough work today that I should be able to sit around."

Because Grady had no other obligations, Chloe had extended the afternoon session as long as she dared, working different muscle groups each time. He had willingly gone along, even though she knew it had to be hard for him. "Like I said, you did good today."

"It will be a long while before I can climb into a saddle."

"You won't be roping any time soon, but riding is certainly not out of the question in time," Chloe said, hoping to encourage him. She guessed it was difficult enough for him to feel disabled. To not be able to ride must feel horrible. Of all the things she'd missed while living in the city, the ability to go out for a ride was one of the biggest.

"If I can get on."

"You're only limited by yourself," she said, taking a sip of her coffee. As soon as the words left her mouth she realized how trite they sounded. "I'm sorry. I shouldn't be mouthing platitudes at you. Occupational hazard."

"Do you enjoy your job?"

"When I'm working, yes. I do."

"How did you get into that line of work?"

"I think part of it was a reaction to what happened to my father."

"He was injured riding his ATV, wasn't he?"

"Which is ironic. He got the thing because he had been thrown from a horse once and didn't want that to happen again." Chloe cradled her warm mug, her thoughts melancholy. "He never got over the injury. I think after losing my mother, and his accident and divorce from Etta, he lost all will to do anything. He just stayed at home, started drinking and things just went downhill from there. Including the ranch. I always wished I could have helped him more, but unfortunately

I had—" She stopped herself there. Grady didn't need to know all the sordid details of her past.

"You had what?" Grady prompted.

"Doesn't matter."

"Does your 'doesn't matter' have anything to do with your ex-husband?"

He was far too astute, Chloe thought.

"Why do you want to know?" she asked, looking down at her cup of coffee, avoiding his direct gaze. Part of her wanted to tell him, to let him know precisely what Jeremy meant to her. Precious little. Even though they had been married for three years, she had felt alone in their relationship for most of that time.

It was that loneliness that made her vulnerable to Grady's attention.

That and the fact Grady was one of the first men in her life to hold her heart. Though she had tried to dismiss her initial attraction to him as a silly schoolgirl crush, images and memories of him had stayed with her the entire time she'd been gone from Little Horn. When she'd found out he had signed up for the army, she'd guessed that she would never see him again. So she had put him out of her life.

Then she had met Jeremy.

"I'm guessing the fact that you, of all people, are now divorced makes it pretty clear that things weren't right between you and your ex-husband. Plus, I'm curious." Grady put his coffee cup down, got to his feet and hobbled over to the fireplace. He knelt and threw on a couple of logs on the fire. Sparks flew up the chimney. He stayed there a moment, looking at her, the fire casting a glow over his handsome face, creating interesting highlights in his sandy brown hair.

For a few precious moments the only sounds were the crackling of the fire in the fireplace and the sighing of the steady wind outside.

"I also want to know what I'm up against," Grady continued.

Chloe's breath caught in her chest like a knot. "What do you mean?" The question was superfluous. She knew exactly what he meant, but she felt she had to try to keep a distance.

Then, to her shock and pleasure, Grady moved to sit beside her on the couch.

"I mean that I want to fill in the gaps between then and now in our lives." He brushed a strand of hair back from her face. His hand lingered on her cheek and she swallowed the attraction she felt building.

"I'm not that interesting and my life with Jeremy—" She stopped there.

"Was what?" he asked. "What was your life with Jeremy like?"

Chloe looked down, her eyelashes shielding her eyes, her lips pressed together.

"Tell me," he whispered, his fingers lightly caressing her cheek.

Shame suffused her at the memory of her marriage, but she also felt a need to unload. To let someone know. Her years with Jeremy had been so lonely. She'd had no mother or father to confide in, and all her friends had been either gone or busy with their own lives.

"He was nice at first. Very charming. But I found out afterward that he was very charming to more women than just me." As she had throughout her marriage, she struggled to separate Jeremy's actions from her life. "I tried to make it work, but it was a failed effort from the start. Jeremy never had any intention of staying faithful. I'm still not sure why he married me."

"Because you're a sweet, caring person," Grady said.

Her heart tilted and she put her hand to her chest as if to hold its errant beat still. Grady was growing harder to resist.

"And that's kind of you to say, but I think he simply saw me as a challenge. I told him the first time we met that I didn't think he was the marrying kind, and he seemed determined to prove me wrong, and I eventually fell for his shtick." It still embarrassed her to admit she was so gullible.

So weak.

"Sorry, I have to go." She swallowed down a sob as shame suffused her.

But Grady's hand was still curled around her neck and he didn't release her.

"What's wrong, Chloe?" His hand was warm, his voice soft and encouraging. "Tell me what's wrong."

Don't look at him, she thought. *Don't give in again.*

"Please?"

It was that single word that broke down her defenses. That word spoken so softly she might have imagined it but for the way his arms tightened around her as if letting her know she was safe.

A word she'd never, ever heard from her ex-husband.

So she gave in.

"Like I told you, we met in a bar," she said. "He was charming. I had just gotten a new job working at a physical therapy clinic, and I had just found out that two of my good friends had gotten engaged. Two others were already married. I guess I wasn't in the best frame of mind to have an attractive man flirting with me. He asked me out and I accepted and soon we were seeing each other regularly.

"Like I said, I made the mistake of telling him I didn't think he was the marrying kind. That's when he turned on the charm. We were married six months after we started dating. Of course it was too quick, but what did I know? I was flattered and I thought he cared about me." She stopped, memories she had suppressed for the past few months returning with a vengeance. Confrontations about his cheating. His lackadaisical attitude. His assurance that if he hadn't married her, no one would have. "It was a mistake that I've regretted ever since."

"Why?"

"It's embarrassing."

Again he said nothing, as if waiting for her to fill the silence. So she did.

"Jeremy cheated on me most of our relationship. I found out afterward that this was going on even before we got married. Information that would have been helpful before I said 'I do' and made promises that I had every intention of keeping and he didn't." She knew it wasn't her fault, but the shame that had filled her when she'd found out how she had been duped returned too easily.

Thankfully Grady said nothing, just held her as if giving her statement weight.

"So you divorced him?"

"I should have. But when I confronted him about his unfaithfulness, he told me he was filing for divorce. He was good friends with a judge and hustled our divorce through the courts. I think he couldn't stand the idea that I might actually divorce him first."

She stopped, thinking of the reason Jeremy had divorced her. He had never wanted children. And she had gotten pregnant.

"The divorce was finalized only two months ago," she continued. "It wasn't what I wanted, but I realized, afterward, it needed to happen."

She stopped there and, as if in response to her declaration the baby she carried moved and Chloe closed her eyes, all the joy in the moment receding. She was carrying another man's baby.

Grady tipped her face up to his. "You don't have to feel ashamed of what happened to you. If anything it has shown me that you are a faithful, caring person." He stroked her face with his fingers, his very touch seeming to ease away her fears. "I think we've both got our stuff to deal with, but I like to believe that we can get through whatever happened. I've discovered one thing since I've come back here. I'm not alone in what I'm dealing with and neither are you. We've got a community and family and support. And we have an amazing life here. I've seen some difficult things to make me realize what we have been blessed with."

She leaned back, her hand still on his chest, keeping the connection between them. "Do you talk about it much? What you saw overseas?"

"Haven't much. I came back to quite a storm of events. Between Vanessa claiming I was Cody's father and Ben's coma and the ranch stuff, I felt as if I had to simply dive in and do what came next."

"Was it hard to come back?"

Grady looked away from her, his eyes taking on a faraway look as if he was returning to Afghanistan. "I saw a lot over there that made me angry, sad, guilty and at the same time so incredibly thankful for the life we have here. It was hard seeing what I saw and experiencing what I did. But I made a decision early on in my career that I wasn't letting my experiences define me. I lost my way from that declaration for a while..." His voice faded.

"You said it once before that you didn't believe God hears prayer," Chloe prompted.

"I think He hears it but I'm not sure what He does about it."

His words bothered her, but she could see that in spite of their harshness he didn't seem entirely convinced of their truth.

"I know it's hard to see God through the storms, but I know He has helped me through many," Chloe said quietly. "I know you had a strong, sincere faith at one time."

Grady sighed. "I did. It's still there, but I'm not so sure God wants me with all the questions I have now. I have to confess I'm struggling right now. Trying to find my footing. In more ways than one," he said with a short laugh.

"'Even strong men stumble,'" Chloe quoted. "I don't think God minds our questions. I think He prefers that to indifference."

Grady seemed to weigh that, his expression serious. "I know that I miss that closeness."

"God is still there, Grady. Maybe you'll just have to move a bit closer yourself and take your questions along."

"I think you might be right," he said.

"I know I've always had to learn that this world is God's. He's ultimately in control. And He's a just God, so sometimes some of the questions will have to wait." She felt as if she was speaking as much to herself as to him. "I know in my heart that while I may wonder where my life is headed, I believe that if I hope in the Lord, like the pastor preached on Sunday, that my strength will be renewed. I think you can believe that, too."

Grady looked down at her, smiling. "You really are amazing."

She tried not to read too much into his comment, into the way his dark brown eyes drew her into their depths, seeming to promise a peace she hadn't felt since her mother died.

Part of her called out a warning. Jeremy, too, had promised much.

But even as the voice reminded her of her past mistakes, she also knew that Grady was nothing like Jeremy.

She knew she could trust him.

"I know I've had to believe that God would lead me through the valleys I've dealt with, as well," she said. Then she gave into an impulse and touched his face, tracing a faint scar on his cheek. The promise that someday she might know the story behind it gave her a gentle thrill.

She wanted to be a part of his life.

Yet her life was such a jumble. She dragged the weight of what had happened to her and she didn't know what to do with it.

She turned to him and as their eyes met she felt as if everything wrong in her life faded away. It was just her and Grady.

To her chagrin, an errant tear slipped down her cheek. She reached up to scrub it away but Grady caught it with his thumb, easing it away.

"Why so sad?"

"Old memories," she said.

He gave her a crooked smile. She felt her resistance ebb like sand before a wave, and before she could say anything more, he bent closer to her, blotting out the light. Then his warm lips were on hers and everything wrong in her life dwindled and died.

* * *

Grady leaned his forehead against Chloe's, his eyes closed, his hands resting on her shoulders. He eased out a sigh, then pulled her against him.

She fit against him as though she belonged, her breath warm on his cheek, her hand resting on his shoulder.

He leaned back against the couch, taking her with him. She nestled in his arms and he pressed a kiss to her forehead, releasing a sigh weighted with many of the losses of the past year.

"I feel as if this has been a long time coming," he said.

"What do you mean?" Her voice was soft, as if hardly daring to disturb the moment.

"I think you know what I'm talking about," he said with a soft chuckle, sensing her question for what it was—a woman's foray into the examination of relationships.

"I do, but I like to talk about it," she said, lifting her head and stroking his hair back from his face, her gesture creating a gentle warmth that he hadn't felt in a long time. As he looked down on her smiling face illuminated by the firelight's glow, he felt, for the first time since he had returned, that he was home. That he was in a place he belonged. He brushed a gentle kiss over her forehead and smiled.

"I've always known who you were," he said, laying his cheek on her head, holding her a bit more tightly as if she might disappear again. "Always been attracted to you, but you never seemed to know I even existed. I remember you talking to my brother and it seemed that you were kind of flirting with him, so I thought he was the one you were interested in."

"I was flirting with Ben?" she said with mock horror. "I thought I was flirting with you all that time."

Grady gave her a gentle shake. "Please tell me you're kidding."

"Of course I am. I could always tell you two apart." Chloe nestled closer, her hand resting on his chest, her finger tracing the line of the buttons on his shirt. "When Ben teased me and I played along, I always hoped you would come and join us and then I could talk to you. You always seemed so aloof, and when Vanessa came I got the feeling you were interested in her."

"That was only because she flirted outrageously with me and you didn't give me any indication that you liked me."

"Classic communication breakdown," she said with a chuckle. "Blame it on me being a bit shy."

"I wonder how things would have turned out

if we had actually talked to each other instead of just assuming things?"

"Guess we'll never know," Chloe said.

"Guess it doesn't matter," Grady returned, fingering her hair away from her face. He brushed another kiss over her forehead and eased out a sigh of satisfaction. "You're here now and so am I, and all the twists and turns of our life led us here."

"I like here," Chloe whispered.

He couldn't stop himself from kissing her again. Then he pulled his head back, his hand cupping her cheek. "So where do we go from here?"

"Seeing as how the roads are glare ice and there's a travel advisory out, nowhere, I guess," she said with a tight smile, deliberately misunderstanding him.

He gave her another gentle shake. "You know what I'm talking about. I don't get the idea that you're a casual person when it comes to relationships."

"I don't know. I did marry Jeremy."

"And you honored your promises even though you knew he wasn't doing the same."

Chloe lowered her gaze, her expression suddenly serious.

"That means more than you can know," Grady said. "You are an honorable person. That's rare."

"Don't give me too much credit," she murmured.

Grady felt a niggle of unease at her words, then realized she was being self-deprecating, which made her even more charming.

"I think I've always admired you," he said, stroking her cheek with his thumb. "While I didn't know exactly what your life with Vanessa was like, I do know that you never spoke ill of her. Never said anything against her while she, on the other hand, seemed to have a more negative attitude."

"That's a kind way to say she didn't like me," Chloe said, smiling again.

"You can joke about that?"

"Now I can," Chloe admitted, laying her hand on his chest. "Listening to her and her mother constantly put down my father was harder, though. I loved my father in spite of his failings."

"You truly are a faithful person," Grady said. "I am so thankful that you came back into my life. You mean more to me than ever before."

"And I'm thankful I'm here," she said.

Then, to his surprise and dismay, another tear slid down her cheek.

"Hey. Babe. What's the matter?" The endearment slipped out even as he touched the track of moisture.

"I don't know," she said, hurriedly swiping away the next tear. "I'm just happy, I guess."

He felt his own heart lift in response. "Me, too," he said, pressing a kiss to her lips. "Me, too."

But as he held her close he realized she hadn't told him the real reason she was crying.

Chapter Eleven

The wind howled around Grady as he made his way across the yard the next morning. His footing was precarious and he slid more times than he cared to count, but thankfully he didn't fall. He pulled his hat down over his ears and tugged up the collar of his jacket, keeping his eyes on the yard light above the door to the barn. Sleet beat at his face and got into his eyes, but finally he made it.

The heavy door slid open and he stepped inside.

He shook the snow off his coat and heard a questioning whinny from the far end of the barn where the horses were kept.

"I'm coming," he called out in answer, shivering as he made his way down the semidark alleyway. He pulled open the door of one of the empty stalls where Josh had stacked some hay. It took him a while to bust open a new bale, but he had time, he told himself.

Though part of him was eager to return to the house.

And Chloe.

He broke loose the bale with his crutch then, grabbed a pitchfork and dumped a few forkfuls into the alleyway, pivoting on his crutch with every movement. When he had enough to feed the horses, he did the same, moving the hay a little more each time. It was tedious and frustrating and he had to fight his annoyance with his limitations.

But he also noticed his hip wasn't as tight as it had been a couple days ago. Though his leg still ached and each movement created a surge of pain, for the first time since his injury he felt a sense of optimism.

Mostly that came from Chloe, who firmly believed that with time and hard work he could regain the majority of his mobility.

He managed to fork the hay into the pens, and when he was done, he was sweating from the exertion.

He dropped onto a bench close to the pens and stretched his leg out in front of him, massaging it to ease the cramp that had come up.

Sweetpea whinnied at him, her head hanging

over the stall as if asking him what he was still doing there.

"I know, Sweetpea. I want to go back to the house, but I need to take a moment," he said, thinking aloud. "Need to figure out where I'm going."

This netted him a faint snort.

"Don't mock me," he said. "I can't just jump into this. Chloe is a wonderful person and she deserves the best. I just don't know if that's me."

Sweetpea just stared at him.

"Plus I've got this ranch and Ben and Mamie..." He felt the weight of each of these obligations, yet even as he listed them he kept thinking about Chloe.

He pulled in a long, slow breath, letting his mind settle, thinking about what she had told him last night. How God welcomed him and his questions.

"I don't know what to do, Lord," he prayed. "I have lots of things I want to ask You about. Things I saw and experienced that I don't know the answers to."

He stopped, feeling a bit foolish, but at the same time feeling a gentle peace surround him.

"I used to be able to talk to You more easily. But I felt as if You didn't listen or didn't care." As he spoke the words aloud, it was as if he heard them for what they were. A lie.

"I guess I know You care. I just wish I could get some direction. Especially now. With Chloe. I feel as if I'm not strong enough to do this."

My hope is only in You, Lord, my solid corner-stone, my strength when I am weak, my help when I'm alone. The words of the song they'd sung last Sunday sifted into his mind.

Maybe he was trying to do too much on his own. Maybe he had to put more of his hope in the Lord.

"Help me to put my life in Your hands, Lord," he prayed. "Help me to put my growing relationship with Chloe there, as well."

He sat a few seconds longer as if to let the prayer soak into his being and returned to the house.

"One final set of stretches and we're done," Chloe said as Grady slowly got off the exercise bike. His range of motion was still restricted, but Chloe could tell that, given time, he would regain more mobility. Maybe not as much as before, but enough to resume most of his former tasks.

"I think I need some encouragement," Grady said, rolling his neck.

"Like what?" she asked, with a teasing smile.

When Grady had come down to the exercise room this morning, he had greeted her with a kiss as natural as breathing. As if they had been dating for months instead of just getting to know each other now.

"I think I could use another kiss," he teased, catching her hand and pulling her close.

Chloe felt her cheeks warm, but she laughed and brushed a kiss over his mouth.

"Oh, c'mon, we're not in junior high." He draped his other hand around her neck and drew her closer yet. His kiss was warm and it gave her exactly the right little thrill.

She pulled back, unable to stop smiling. This morning at breakfast she and Grady had sat side by side, their hands twined together under the table. Mamie had sat across from them looking quite self-satisfied and healthy. Once again Chloe doubted her story about how ill she felt, but she wasn't about to challenge her. She had guessed Mamie had ulterior motives for hiring her in the first place, but right about now, she didn't care.

"Does that help?"

"Immensely," he said. "Now what am I supposed to do?"

"Lie down, arms beside you, and I'll tell you." She walked him through the series, correcting his movements as he worked. "Just make sure you don't push too hard," Chloe warned as he completed the last set. "You don't want to strain your muscles and put yourself back."

"Guess I just want to get better quick." Grady

finished, then dropped onto his back on the exercise mat, one arm flung over his eyes. "I'm an impatient man."

"That could be a detriment," Chloe said, kneeling beside him. "Patience is the main ingredient in any therapy program."

"You always have an answer," he groaned as she twisted his leg just enough to stretch the calf muscles.

"We get an app when we graduate that we put on our smartphones as well as a book that matches comment to complaint," she said, settling back on her haunches while Grady rolled over and got to his feet. He wavered as he reached for his crutch, but she didn't help him, knowing how independent he was. As long as it didn't look as though he would fall she knew enough to leave him alone. "I've used it many times with some of my more reluctant clients."

"You've had clients more reluctant than me?"

"Oh, yes," she said with a definite nod. "There are more people who don't like to acknowledge they need help."

"It's hard," he said. "I think I was dealing with false pride." He gave her a sheepish smile. "I didn't want to admit in front of you that I wasn't as strong as I used to be. That I was weak."

"I've always thought that it takes great strength of character for anyone to recognize honestly what they can and can't do." She gave him an encouraging smile. "Some take longer than others, but you did come to that point, and I think that's honorable and manly."

"I think what I struggled with most was I felt I wasn't the man I used to be."

"None of us are what we used to be," she said, cleaning up the equipment she had used today with a spray bottle. "We've both come through our lives with wounds, mental as well as physical."

"What wounds do you carry?"

Her heart suddenly felt as though it was pushing heavily against her chest, filling it with its racing beat. She took a slow breath. She had put this off too long. It was time to tell him the truth. She clutched the bottle, her back to him, steadying her breath, readying herself. But the sound of the baby crying broke into the moment.

Chloe spun around just as Mamie came into the room holding a red-faced, screaming Cody, whose cries filled the room. "I'm sorry, Chloe. I don't know what's wrong with him. He just woke up. I know he's supposed to be sleeping a bit longer."

"No need to be sorry," Chloe said, hurrying to take the squalling infant from her. "I'm sorry I wasn't there to help."

"Working with Grady is as much your job as taking care of this little one," Mamie said, handing Cody over. "So you have nothing to apologize for."

Chloe settled Cody against her, rocking him, shushing him, stroking his warm, damp head. Immediately his cries eased into hiccups and he lay his head against her shoulder.

"You certainly have a way with him," Mamie said with admiration. "A natural mother."

It was a simple, innocent comment, but it was a reminder of what she had yet to tell Grady.

Not yet, she thought. *Not yet.* She didn't want anything to upset what was happening between them. Part of her felt dishonest, but she simply wanted the ordinary time of being with Grady without all the complications that would come with her news. She knew things were growing, moving to a serious, solid place. She just wanted them both to have their footing before she created more instability.

Isn't that a bit self-serving?

Chloe stifled that unrelenting voice. It wasn't selfish, she reasoned. It was practical.

"I'll go take care of Cody," Chloe said, turning to Grady. "You're okay for now?"

He gave her a discreet wink. "More than okay."

Chloe blushed again. Tucking Cody against her, she turned and followed Mamie up the stairs. She sensed that the older woman wanted to say something, but Chloe wasn't ready to bring out into the cold light of day what was growing between her and Grady. It was so new, so tender. Something she had yearned for, for so many years, and she was afraid too much dissemination could destroy its fragile fabric.

So she just kept going up, bringing Cody to the nursery. She lay the little boy on the changing table, smiling at him as he gave her a drooling grin, his cupid's-bow lips glistening.

"You are a little stinker, aren't you?" she cooed as she took off his pants and changed his diaper. He had a rash, which, Chloe suspected, had woken him in the first place.

Outside, the storm, which hadn't abated since it had begun, roared on, pelting the window with snow mixed with rain. Chloe felt safe in this place. Centered. As though this was where she was meant to be.

She got Cody cleaned up, then sat in the rocking chair in one corner of the nursery cuddling him and trying to ease him into sleep. His warm body melted against hers and she felt a flush of maternal joy. What would it be like to hold her own baby?

Her heart clenched at the thought. Where would she be when that happened? Here? With Grady?

Somewhere else?

Help me, Lord, she prayed, fear wrapping an

icy fist around her heart. *Help me to do the right thing. To find the right time to tell him. Please help Grady to understand.*

The thought that he might not was too diffi-cult to contemplate. For the first time in her life she felt as if the boundaries of her life were fall-ing into pleasant places. She was back in Little Horn, and the man she had spun so many dreams around had kissed her. Had told her how much she meant to him.

Did she dare disrupt that?

You'll have to sooner than later. You can't hide that pregnancy forever.

"Please help him understand," she prayed aloud, holding Cody even closer, feeling sorry for this poor child who didn't know his mother and whose father was still unconscious. "And be with Ben," she continued. "Please return him to this family."

She eased out a gentle sigh, rocking the little baby, singing to him and her own child at the same time.

From below she heard Grady and Mamie's murmured conversation, then the sound of the shower running. The ordinary sounds of a house-hold. A home.

Cody finally fell asleep and Chloe laid him gently in his crib, stroking the little one's downy head. "Sleep tight, little one. May God watch over you," she whispered.

And me, as well, she added.

She left the room, gently closing the door behind her. When she arrived downstairs she saw Mamie pulling out her bread pans.

"Here, let me do that," Chloe said, hurrying over to her side. "You rest. You're still recuperating, I'm sure. Did you want some tea?"

"Yes of course. Tea would be lovely," Mamie said hurriedly, dropping onto a nearby stool and sighing as if she had to remind herself how ill she was supposed to be. Chloe stifled a smile.

Chloe plugged in the electric kettle and looked out the window over the yard. She could barely see the barn through the storm and once again was thankful she didn't have to go outside. Thankful for this place of shelter and refuge.

She looked over the bread recipe, humming as she gathered the ingredients.

"You seem happy," Mamie said as the water began to boil.

"I guess I am," Chloe said, her cheeks flushing as she guessed that Mamie knew exactly what the reason for her lighthearted attitude was.

"So does Grady. Not only that, he seems content. Something I haven't seen in him for a while."

Chloe felt the weight of that statement, as if

Mamie was hinting that she might be the reason for that.

"I'm glad. He's making decent progress. Of course, we've only just started, but he's determined to do well, and that means he probably will. It took a while to convince him, but I think he's motivated now."

"Of course he is," Mamie said with a smug tone. "He has the best reason in the world to improve himself now."

Chloe wasn't sure what to say to that leading statement.

"I know my grandson may not always be the most cooperative," Mamie said. "But he's a good man."

Chloe looked over at her, realizing that Mamie knew exactly what had been going on.

"He is," Chloe agreed. "The best."

This was exactly the right answer, judging from Mamie's smug look.

When the water boiled Chloe made tea, poured a cup for Mamie and herself and returned to mixing up the ingredients. The yeast had soaked long enough and she could add the rest. Thankfully Mamie found a magazine and paged through it as she drank her tea, not saying anything more and leaving Chloe to work in quiet. As she cracked eggs and added oil to the bread dough, Chloe felt a curious peace slip over her. It had been years since she had done any baking. Jeremy had been seldom at home to eat it and when she had attended school, she hadn't had time.

She turned on the mixer to knead the dough just as Grady came into the kitchen.

Chloe felt her heart skip a beat when she saw him cleaned up, his hair still damp from his shower, cheeks shining from his shave. And when his dark eyes found hers, locking on to her gaze, she felt a sense of homecoming.

This is right, she thought. *This fits. This is where I belong. Everything else will come together.*

It had to.

Chapter Twelve

The next morning, Grady got up, stretched and then groaned as he felt muscles he had forgotten were part of his anatomy. He was even more stiff and sore than yesterday. But it was a good sore. The kind he used to feel after a hard workout.

He rolled his neck and beyond the door of his bedroom he could hear Cody banging his spoon on the high chair and Chloe talking to him in lilting tones. He felt a surge of happiness he hadn't felt in years.

He was home, and the woman he cared about more with each passing minute was under the same roof. These past few days had given them a time out of time. An opportunity to simply be together without all the complications of the outside world.

Then he heard it.

Silence. He walked to the window and pushed

aside the curtain, lifted the blinds. Gray clouds still blanketed the sky, but the storm had passed. No wind blew; no snow slanted sideways over the yard. All was calm.

Which meant that soon life would return to normal.

He felt a touch of concern at the thought. What would happen to him and Chloe then?

Then he laughed that foolish idea off. As if their changing feelings could only thrive in this little bit of space and time they had been granted. He'd cared for her before, and he knew she had cared for him, as well. He felt in his heart that what he and Chloe had would only grow.

To where?

The question hovered, creating both concern and anticipation. He knew he wanted more than simply to date Chloe. Though what was happening between them had come up quickly, he also knew she wasn't a casual dater, either.

He looked out over the yard at the ranch he and his brother had inherited. A legacy going back many generations. Though he had given so much of his life to the military, he'd never realized how important this place was to him until now.

And to the life he could give any future family.

He got dressed quickly, finding his crutch, praying that someday he wouldn't need it anymore, then made his way to the kitchen and Chloe.

Warmth braided with delicious smells greeted him as he stepped into the kitchen.

His grandmother sat on the other side of the table drinking a mug of tea, paging through a magazine. A batch of cinnamon buns, the reason for the home smells, lay cooling on the counter. Chloe was trying to coax breakfast into Cody's cereal-encrusted mouth. The little guy was banging a spoon on the tray of the high chair, babbling his pleasure. His hair stuck up, and when Chloe held a spoon of food in front of him he batted it away, netting a smile from Chloe instead of a reprimand.

She was so incredibly patient, he thought, watching as she wiped the cereal from the high chair and from her arm with a cloth.

"Are you done, munchkin?" she asked, wiping his mouth, as well. "I hope so because I'm ready to eat, too."

"I'm hoping those cinnamon buns are for breakfast," he said, popping a new pod in the coffeemaker.

Chloe spun around, and when she saw him her bright smile warmed his heart.

"Good morning," she said.

"Chloe made them," his grandmother piped up.

"You must have been up before dawn," Grady said, grabbing a mug out of the cupboard and flashing her a warm smile.

"They're overnight cinnamon buns," she said. "I haven't made them for years. But I'm sure they're fine."

"I'm sure they are, too," Grady said. The coffeemaker burbled, pouring a stream of brown liquid into his mug. "Looks as if the storm has cleared. Things should be getting back to normal soon."

"That's good, I suppose," his grandmother said. "I imagine you'll be back to work once the roads clear."

"I'll have to. After breakfast I'd like to check on the horses again." Then, just to see what his grandmother would do, he stopped by Chloe and pressed a kiss to her soft, warm neck. "Good morning," he whispered.

She ducked her head, but he caught the edge of her smile then looked over at his grandmother, who grinned like the Cheshire cat.

Breakfast was a quiet affair. Cody sat on Chloe's lap as she ate, watching Grady as if trying to figure out what he should think of him. Mamie made small talk. Chloe gave Grady a shy look from time to time.

When breakfast was over, Chloe sat Cody in his chair and started clearing the table. But Mamie stopped her. "You just go and change Cody. I'll clean up and then watch him. You should go help Grady in the barn."

"He's been managing the past few days without me—"

"I wouldn't mind the extra help," Grady interrupted before Chloe could formulate a reason not to come. He guessed she was trying to be all noble and responsible, but if Grandma wanted to give them a few moments alone, he was taking them. Once the roads were cleared, the ranch hands would be back, then Maddy Coles and the other girls would return and there would be precious few quiet moments for them. "I'd like to check on the other horses outside as well, and I'd like your help for that."

"In that case, I'll take care of Cody and be ready in fifteen minutes."

It was actually five, which made Grady smile. It seemed Chloe was as eager as he was to spend time together.

The air still held a hint of moisture as they walked across the icy yard. Grady took his time, his steps deliberate. There was no way he was falling down in front of Chloe. When he went out on his own to feed the horses, he didn't care as much about finesse. He had slipped and slid, but that hadn't mattered. He hadn't had an audience then.

Now, he knew he was being proud, and Chloe had seen him at his weakest, but he still felt the need to show her that he was capable.

The barn was silent when they stepped inside, then Sweetpea whinnied at them followed by Babe and Shiloh.

"They're probably hungry," Grady said, his halting steps echoing in the cavernous barn.

"Do you want me to help feed them?"

"Nah. I'll be okay." He had things down to a system and though it took time, he wasn't as ungainly as he had been the first time he'd done it.

Sweetpea, Babe and Shiloh hung their heads over the gates of their pens, watching patiently as he approached them. "Hey, girls," he said. "How are you doing?"

They whinnied back, their replies echoing through the barn.

"You care to translate?" Chloe teased.

Grady pushed open the door of the stall holding the hay with his crutch and shot her a grin over his shoulder. "Sweetpea is asking me why I had to bring that gorgeous girl in here, and Babe is asking me where her breakfast is. Very selfish, that one. Shiloh is just curious."

Chloe laughed at his lame comments, making him feel as if he might actually own a sense of humor.

She walked over to Babe, stroked the horse's head. "Your meal will come in good time," she said.

Grady tried not to rush. His pride made him

want to look competent in front of Chloe, but his more practical nature reminded him to take his time. If he fell down again, he'd look even more foolish.

Then, without saying anything, Chloe walked into the pen where the hay was, grabbed another fork and stabbed it into the bale. She brought it over to Babe and dumped it into the stall. Then went back for another. Grady bit back his protest, knowing on one level he should be happy for the help. The less time he spent awkwardly making his way back and forth with the hay, the less chance he had of falling or embarrassing himself. And Chloe knew what she was doing.

A few minutes later they were done, the horses munching loudly.

"Amazing how they can make that dry old hay seem so tasty," Chloe said, hanging over Babe's stall, watching her eat.

Grady set aside the fork and while she was looking at Babe, stretched out a kink in his leg, grimacing at the sudden and unexpected stab of pain. He tried not to feel disheartened, knowing it would take months before the pain would ease off. Chloe hadn't promised him any sudden recuperation, and he knew better than to expect that, but it was still frustrating to be so hampered in what he could do when he wanted to show how capable he was.

"When are they supposed to foal?" Chloe asked, joining him on the bench by the stalls.

"Sweetpea is due in April, Babe and Shiloh in May."

"I remember we had one mare who had a foal. I named and raised her. Saul helped me train her. He also tried to talk me out of calling her Shayalama. Said it would take me too long to train her because it would take me too long to say her name every time I wanted her to do something."

Grady smiled, though he heard the hint of sorrow in her voice. "What happened to this Shayalama?"

"She was sold when things went bad for my father." She rested her elbows on her knees, her chin in her hands, her eyes seeming to be looking to another place.

Grady stroked her shoulder in commiseration. "That must have been a hard time for you."

"I was gone for the worst of the decline. Which brings its own load of guilt. The last few years, when things got really bad, I was…" Her voice drifted off and she pressed her lips together.

"You were married to Jeremy."

She nodded, giving him a rueful smile. "I should have paid more attention to what was happening. I should have helped my father more. His life was so scattered."

"I know how you feel," Grady said. "I had the

same difficulty with Ben. Being away, yet knowing what kind of life he was living. I guess I shouldn't have been as angry as I was with him."

"It's hard to watch someone make bad choices."

"I didn't need to be as hard on him as I was."

"You did it because he matters to you," Chloe said, turning back to him, taking his hand in hers. "In our studies we talked about the special bond that twins share. I think you become more invested in each other's lives. And as a result, you probably care more. You told him what you did because you love him, not because you wanted to be some kind of policeman."

Grady squeezed her hand in response, chuckling in spite of his regrets. "You are so perceptive. That's exactly what Ben had accused me of doing. In fact, he informed me that I was a soldier, not a cop."

"I guess we're on the same wavelength, too," she joked.

He curled his hand around her neck, pulling her in for another kiss. "I'd like to think so."

She lay against him with a gentle sigh, her hand resting on his chest, her other around his waist. "I like this place."

"This barn?" he said, deliberately misunderstanding her.

"Being in your arms in this barn," she said with a chuckle. "I like being here on the ranch."

"Do you miss your work?"

"It was what I trained for. I hope that someday I will be able to do it full-time again."

Her comment reminded him that her stay here was temporary. Did he dare assume she would want to make it permanent?

The thought jolted him. Was he ready to make that commitment?

Was she?

The stillness of the barn, broken only by the munching of the horses, made Chloe feel a gentle push-pull of emotions. Grady's appeal; the reality of the baby she carried. The honesty they had just shared; the secret she held close.

She had to tell him before she moved so far down this path she couldn't find her way back.

Her heart stepped up its tempo as she scrambled for the right words to convey the information, the right time.

Now, her mind told her.

Later, said her heart.

"I guess we should get back to the house," Grady said, breaking the soft silence with his comment. "Don't want Grandma to worry about us."

"I doubt she's worried," Chloe said, feeling the relief of the momentary reprieve.

"You're probably right. In fact, I think that

Mamie's illness was either contrived or exaggerated."

"And why would she do that?" Chloe asked.

Grady gave her a conspiratorial smile. "So that we could do this." He gave her another kiss.

Was this really her? Chloe thought as she drew back from him, her hand on his shoulder, her eyes locked with his. Was this really Chloe Miner kissing Grady Stillwater for real instead of those endless fantasies she had spun up in her room, hugging her pillow, pretending it was him?

"I like doing this," she said. Then she kissed him back. For real.

"I do, too, but I should get hold of Josh, Emilio or Lucas and see which of them can come in. The cows will need to be fed either today or tomorrow."

So soon, Chloe thought. So soon the outside world would descend into their lives with obligations and ordinariness.

But who know what would come with it?

Grady grabbed his crutch and stood, his movements awkward. Chloe suspected most of his stiffness resulted from the workouts she had done with him. Had she pushed him too hard?

"I should go visit Ben as soon as possible," Grady said as he set his crutch under his arm. "I hope he doesn't feel as if we've abandoned him."

"Just tell him what happened. He'll understand."

"I love how you talk about Ben as though he knows exactly what is going on."

"Like I said, it's subliminal. He might not remember, but I believe it enters his subconscious and takes root there."

"I guess sooner or later we'll have to tell him about Cody," Grady said as they made their way to the door.

"I wish I could tell you when the right time to do that is."

"I know. I don't want him to feel as shocked as I did when I heard that Vanessa was parading Cody around town telling everyone I was the father." He pulled open the large sliding door, the outside light a sharp brightness compared to the gloom of the barn. "I tell you, much as I love that little guy, I am thankful he's Ben's child." He gave her a warm smile, touching her cheek. "Starting a relationship with the responsibility of a child is a heavy, difficult thing to deal with."

Chloe blinked in the bright sunlight, cold blooming in her chest, spreading to her hands, her head, her feet.

Her first response was flight. Run. Get away from the words that chilled her soul.

The responsibility of a child. Heavy, difficult thing to deal with.

His words wound around her heart like an icy fist.

Good thing you didn't tell him about the baby.

She hurried ahead on the ice, her feet slipping in her rush, but thankfully she didn't fall.

"Chloe? What's wrong?" Grady called out behind her.

But she kept going, the house ahead of her. Sanctuary.

"Chloe," Grady called again.

Then she heard a clatter as his crutch fell, a muffled thump and Grady's cry of pain.

She spun around in time to see Grady sprawled out on the ground, his one leg at an awkward angle.

"No, oh, no," she cried, hurrying to his side, hoping, praying that he hadn't done more damage to his injured leg.

She dropped to her knees beside him as Grady scrambled, trying to regain his footing.

"Here. Let me help," she said, fitting her shoulder under his armpit as she had been taught.

Grady groaned and Chloe felt another flicker of regret. But even as she helped him to his feet, she knew that as soon as she could, she would retreat to her room. For now, however, she was Grady's physical therapist and she had to help him get back up.

"You okay to stand?" she asked as they managed to get up.

He simply nodded and she got his crutch and

handed it to him. He didn't look at her as he stumbled toward the house. He was probably in pain, but she also knew Grady well enough that he would never admit it. Especially not to her.

However, she was in pain as well, and every moment walking alongside him created her own agony.

With each hesitant step his words reverberated through her mind. *Heavy thing. Heavy thing.*

Too heavy for him, it seemed.

They got to the house, and as soon as they were inside Chloe made her escape, mumbling some excuse to find Cody, even though Mamie told them he was sleeping.

Chloe said no to coffee, the thought of sitting down with Grady and Mamie and acting as if all was well unbearable. She hurried upstairs, her feet unable to move fast enough.

Difficult thing to deal with...responsibility of a child...heavy...difficult. At least she had kept her secret to herself.

She dropped into the rocking chair in the nursery and lay her head back, ignoring the moisture trickling down her cheeks. Now what was she supposed to do? If Grady had a hard enough time thinking about taking on Cody, whom, for a moment, everyone thought was his, how could she expect him to take on another man's child?

A man who was less than honorable. A man

who had easily renounced any claim to his own biological child, then disappeared.

She closed her eyes, rocking, praying in snatches, sending out ragged petitions consisting of only two words. *Help. Me.*

Cody stirred in the crib and she got up to check on him, but he dropped back into the deep, innocent sleep of a baby, his lashes resting on his chubby cheeks, one dimpled hand beside his head.

Chloe stood over his crib a moment, her hand splayed over her own stomach as if protecting the child who grew within.

"Guess it's just you and me," she whispered, her sorrow threatening to choke her as she returned to the chair and her rocking.

And now what? How could she continue to work with Grady knowing how he felt? Knowing that if he found out about her baby he would surely reject her to her face?

She couldn't bear that.

But how could she leave Cody? The poor child had already been through so much. Another change would be detrimental.

And where would she go if she left? She had no job, no home. She pressed her hands to her stomach, her mind churning as she tried to think of where in this cold, unfriendly world she was supposed to find sanctuary for herself and her baby.

She closed her eyes and as she rocked, her prayers were sent up.

Help me to trust, Lord, that You will bring me where I should be. Help me to love this child and to love You. To put my life in Your hands.

And help me not to cry the next time I see Grady.

Chapter Thirteen

"Are you feeling okay?" Mamie asked Grady as he straggled into the kitchen the next morning. "I saved some breakfast for you." She glanced at the clock, an old habit of hers when the boys had had an especially late night. Her quiet reprimand.

Grady knew exactly what time it was. It had surprised him as well when he'd looked at the clock this morning. Nine. Meant he had lost half the morning already.

"I'm fine. I'm tired," he said.

Exhausted would be a better word. He hadn't fallen asleep until about four this morning, his mind going over and over what happened yesterday.

After he had fallen on the ice, Chloe had found all kinds of reasons to avoid him the rest of the day, telling Mamie, not him, that she wasn't feeling well.

He knew she was fine. Or had been fine as they talked in the barn, edging toward vague plans, hesitantly delineating the parameters of their relationship.

He'd thought they had been getting somewhere. And then he'd fallen.

She'd seen him helpless before. It was this helplessness he wanted to hide from her, hence his reluctance to do physical therapy with her. But he had given in and she'd helped him, seen him at his weakest.

But then, with startling clarity, he realized she had never seen him fall before. Had never seen him sprawled on the ground like some landed fish flopping around. He tried to dismiss the picture, but he couldn't lose the idea that Chloe had backed away from him because of it.

His mother hadn't been able to deal with his father's disability. Had seeing him on the ground reminded Chloe exactly how weak he truly was?

Part of him didn't want to believe that of her, but it was the only explanation for her sudden retreat.

"Did Chloe say what she was doing today?"

Mamie shot him a sharp look, as if he should know this himself.

"She said she was taking Cody out for a walk with his little sleigh down the south ridge now that the weather has cleared. Are the boys coming back today?"

"Last night I called Lucas and Emilio and sent a text to Josh, and so far they're all able to come. I think the girls should wait a day or two yet." He rubbed his forehead, thinking of all the work that needed to be done now that things were getting back to normal. "Is Martha Rose coming back?"

"I hope so. If the boys are back, they'll need meals made, and I don't have the energy or time." She sighed lightly and Grady shot her a look of concern. His grandmother had always seemed indestructible, but he'd noticed she wasn't as spry as she once was. One more concern on his mind.

As he put on his coat to leave for the barn, he heard footsteps coming down the stairs and his heart jumped as he heard Chloe talking to Mamie. "Just thought I would let you know I'm taking Cody out now."

His grandmother's reply was an indistinct murmur. Grady quickly buttoned up his coat, then realized to his dismay that he had left his crutch leaning against the counter in the kitchen. He knew he couldn't navigate the still slippery yard without it, but he didn't want to go back to get it and face Chloe.

He was about to leave anyway when he heard footsteps again. And there was Chloe, holding his crutch out to him, a stark reminder if ever there was one. "You forgot this," she said not meeting his eyes, her voice cool.

He took it, questions burning in his chest, pride keeping them unvoiced.

"And I won't be able to do therapy with you this afternoon," she said, her hands folded primly in front of her, a protective gesture.

"That works out good," he replied. "I'll be busy all day." Yesterday he had been looking forward to another therapy session with her. To pushing himself again, to showing her what he was willing to try.

But not now. Not with her expression so cool and reserved.

With a murmured thanks he made his way past her, resisting the urge to look back. He didn't want to know if she was watching him, but he acted as if she was, taking his time, taking cautious steps. As he walked, his mind ticked back to a comment she had made that he had overheard. *...couldn't give him what she needed and what woman can live like that?*

And as an icy claw gripped his chest, he paused, unable to walk for a moment.

So that was what this was all about. Her retreat. Her silence. She realized she couldn't live like *that*. Just like his mother couldn't. Like Etta Vane couldn't.

He finally got to the barn, thankfully without

falling or even slipping, and once inside he leaned against the door, his emotions a swirl of confusion, anger and sorrow at the injury that had incapacitated him. The disability that had made him less of a man. Just like his father.

"Boss? Is that you?"

Josh poked his head out of Sweetpea's stall.

"Yeah. I'm here. You're here early."

"Just wanted to make sure everything was okay. What with you laid up and all."

"I'm hardly laid up," Grady snapped, feeling overly testy, and then immediately feeling bad when he saw the surprise on his hired hand's face. "Sorry, Josh. Didn't sleep well last night, so I'm a bit short this morning."

"At six foot some, no one could call you short," Josh said with a laugh, in one comment acknowledging and dismissing Grady's apology. "So I figured we need to get those cows fed and see how the horses are," Josh said. "I should also check those cameras."

"I doubt the thieves were out and about during the storm," Grady said.

"Yeah, but it wouldn't hurt to make sure they're all still working."

"Have you heard about any more thefts?"

Josh shook his head. "Nope. But then, like you said, with the storm and all maybe the thieves decided not to risk anything the past few days. What else is on the list for today?"

"The Massey tractor needs some work on the bale forks before you feed, and the John Deere needs an oil change. I was hoping to get it done this week, but didn't feel like tackling it on my own."

"Are we getting muffins again this morning?" Josh asked with a hopeful gleam in his eye.

"Unless Martha Rose makes it back here, I doubt it."

"Chloe's busy?"

"Yeah." And that was all he was saying about that.

Chloe trudged over the snow, pulling Cody behind her on the sled. His happy squeals were the perfect antidote for the knot that tightened with each minute she was apart from Grady.

The sun was shining, promising hope, but Chloe couldn't find it to latch on to it. Hope seemed as far away as summer did right now. She shivered and looked back at Cody all bundled up, his stocking cap sitting crooked over his face, obscuring one eye. But he was waving his arms, laughing at everything he saw.

"You are so adorable," she said, feeling a motherly burst of affection for him. He laughed at her as if he agreed, then suddenly leaned over in the sled, looking past her.

Chloe couldn't stop the lift of her heart at the thought that it might be Grady, but when she turned it was only Emilio walking toward her, carrying a large envelope. Even though the air was still cold enough to turn his breath into vapor, he wore his coat open, and only a shabby straw cowboy hat on his head.

"Hey, Chloe. Grady told me I might find you out here," he said as he came near.

Chloe's heart jumped just a bit thinking Grady had been watching her, then she realized that Mamie must have told him.

"I was just taking Cody out on his sleigh. It's so nice."

"So glad the weather turned decent. I was getting worried about you guys stuck out here, and Grady and all, but I'm sure you managed just fine." He gave her a gap-toothed grin, as if sharing some inside joke, then knelt to tickle Cody under the chin with one large, grease-streaked finger. "Hey, little guy. You having fun with Chloe here? You making sure she and Grady behave themselves?"

His innocent words, assuming a relationship between her and Grady, hit her like hammer blows.

It won't happen, she thought, despair tugging at her.

She couldn't give in, however. She had to think of her baby and what was best for him or her.

"I got something for you," Emilio said, straightening and handing her the large envelope. "Grady asked me to pick up the mail while I was coming through town and this came for you. Whoever it was knows you're staying here, I guess."

Chloe frowned as she took the large, heavy envelope with her name scrawled across the front. The only attempt at an address was "Chlo at Stillwater Ranch," and there was no return address anywhere on the envelope. Her name was misspelled, so whoever had sent it didn't know her well.

"Looks mysterious," Emilio said with a wink.

"It certainly does," Chloe agreed. "Thanks for getting it for me."

"No problem. You coming to see Grady? He and Josh are working on the tractor. I'm sure he won't mind if you stop by." His assumption of a relationship was like another hook in her heart.

"I should bring Cody back to the house and find out what's in here," she said with a forced smile, holding the envelope aloft.

"Are you bringing muffins later?"

"No. I'm…busy. I promised Mamie I would help…help her…with her knitting." Chloe floundered around, scrambling for any kind of excuse.

"Well, I'll tell Grady you said hey."

"That's not necessary," Chloe said with a dismissive wave of her hand.

Emilio looked puzzled, then shrugged. "Sure. Well, see you around." He waggled his fingers at Cody, then sauntered off, hands jammed in the pocket of his jacket, whistling as he walked.

She had to leave, Chloe thought as she turned and trudged back to the house. It was as if every encounter was a stark reminder of what she could never have.

...starting a relationship with the responsibility of a child...heavy thing.

All night Grady's words had resonated through her mind, circling like ravens, pecking at her insecurities.

She was a divorced woman, carrying another man's child.

She was fairly sure a man of honor, a soldier such as Grady, would struggle with that idea, especially when she had told him the exact state of her marriage to Jeremy.

The house was quiet when she stepped inside. Mamie must be sleeping, and it didn't sound as if Martha Rose was here yet. So she took Cody upstairs, changed him and played with him until he started rubbing his ears and fussing. Then she laid him down, sang him to sleep and retreated to her room.

Once there she took out her Bible, needing

comfort and spiritual nourishment. Needing the reminder of God's faithfulness.

Her hands turned to Lamentations, easily finding the passage in chapter three that she had drawn from so often.

"The steadfast love of the Lord never ceases; His mercies never come to an end; they are new every morning; great is Your faithfulness."

She had clung to these very promises of God's faithfulness through all the years she had been married to Jeremy, struggling to stay true to her vows when she knew her husband wasn't. The promise of God's faithfulness had helped her then, and she prayed it would help now. God's love was all encompassing and faithful and unending.

She closed her eyes, pressing the palms of her hands against her cheeks, trying not to let fear and despair take over, trying not to think of what she had lost with Grady. Instead, she tried to remind herself that God's love was sufficient for her.

"Please help me to hold on to that," she whispered, continuing her prayer, praying for her baby, for Ben, for the people of the community and finally for continued healing for Grady.

She knew he needed to continue his physical therapy sessions, but she also knew she couldn't work with him.

Not anymore.

She finished her prayers just as her phone rang. It was Lucy.

"Hey there," Chloe said, leaning back against the head of her bed, tucking her legs under her. "What's up?"

"Thankfully not much, what with the storm and all. No thefts and no gifts."

Which made Chloe suddenly remember the letter she had received. She had left it in Cody's room. "I got something this morning that seemed a little odd," she said, getting up and slipping into Cody's room, glad for the distraction from Grady and the sorrow clinging to her.

"What is it?"

"Just a minute," Chloe whispered, picking up the envelope and checking on the little boy. He lay with his head to one side, his chubby cheeks pink from the cold, his tiny hand curled up beside his head. Her heart wavered at the sight, then she quickly left, hurrying back to her own room.

"Are you still there?"

"Yeah. I just got the letter from Cody's room."

"Letter? Who from?"

"No return address and it was sent to me via the Stillwater ranch. Whoever sent it spelled my name wrong, so that could be a clue." Chloe sat cross-legged on her bed, phone tucked under her ear as she slit open the envelope. Another envelope, thick and heavy, fell out as she pulled a single piece of paper out.

"What's inside?"

"A letter…" Chloe scanned over the contents. "From Robin Hood, apparently. He's giving me a little something to help me with my dream of staring up a physical therapy clinic." Chloe frowned, read the letter again.

"Is it handwritten?"

"No. Typed. Not signed, obviously. Probably printed on a computer…and now I've put my fingerprints all over it."

"Relax. This isn't *CSI: Little Horn*," Lucy said with a light chuckle. "I doubt I would be able to figure out whose prints they are if they're not in any criminal database. But I need to see it. What's in the envelope?" she asked, just as Chloe picked it up and carefully peeled it open.

A huge stack of one-hundred-dollar bills fell out. Chloe's mouth fell open as she stared at the cash now spilled on her bed.

"Money. Hundreds of dollars." She did a quick calculation, flicking through the bills. "Nearest I can tell it's close to about ten thousand dollars."

Adrenaline mixed with fear shot through her veins. How had this person known about her dream? How had he tracked her down here?

"This creeps me out," Chloe said, pushing the

money away from her as if it might contaminate her.

"No kidding. But you know you can't keep the money."

"I don't even want it," Chloe said, staring at the pile of bills, her arms wrapped around her legs. "Who could have known about this?"

"Grady?"

"I doubt he would resort to this," Chloe said.

"I think you're right. But like I said, you have to give the money up. Carson has called an unexpected meeting of the cowboy league this Saturday. Grady will have to sit in as Ben's replacement. You could give the money to him to give to me then."

"Sure. I can do that." She could give it to Mamie, she figured. Mamie could hand it over. She didn't want to face Grady. Not if she could avoid it.

"By the way, how is that handsome soldier?"

Lucy's innocent question created an ache in Chloe's heart.

"He's…he's…good."

"Good? Be still my heart. That's all you can say about the guy you've loved since grade school?"

Chloe drew in a slow breath, trying to stay on top of her scattered emotions. She didn't want this taking over her life. "I don't want to talk about him."

A beat of silence greeted that statement. "Since when? I know you're attracted to him. You two just spent three days all secluded from the outside world with only an older woman and a baby. Don't tell me that something didn't happen?"

"Something did." The comment burst out of her, the need to share what she was dealing with overcoming her natural reticence. So she told Lucy, "He kissed me. I kissed him."

"What? That's amazing. I'm so happy for you." Her enthusiasm was like salt on the wound.

"So things are moving forward?" Lucy continued. "I know you've always liked him."

"I have. I do." She released a short laugh. "I've never cared for anyone the way I care for Grady. And I thought things were getting somewhere."

"Thought? What happened?"

Chloe cradled her stomach with her arm, as if assuring her baby of her love. "He made a comment about kids. How glad he was that Cody wasn't his. That he couldn't think about starting a relationship with the responsibility of a child."

"So why is that a problem?"

Chloe looked down at her stomach, and in spite of everything that had happened the past while, she felt a smile curve her lips. Life was growing inside her. A baby was developing. Flesh of her flesh.

She knew she could keep the secret no longer.

"I'm pregnant. That's the problem."

Another time Lucy's gasp would have created a surge of shame, but Chloe couldn't allow that to happen. She was this child's mother. Its first line of defense.

You and me against the world, she thought.

"Jeremy is the father," she continued.

"Oh, Chloe…"

"And once we got divorced, he ducked out. Haven't heard anything from him, and I don't know where he is. Part of me doesn't want him in my child's life, but the fact that he would abandon us like that makes me so furious."

"Oh, sweetie," Lucy murmured. "I wish you would have told me sooner."

"I was ashamed at first, and I wasn't sure exactly how to tell you."

"I wish I could come over."

"No. It's fine. You're busy enough with everything that's been going on."

Lucy's tired sigh underlined Chloe's assumption. "I am. It's taking over my life, and people are starting to ask for my badge. I just wish I could crack this thing."

"You will. You just need one good break."

"Is that a pun?"

Chloe chuckled. "Not intentional."

"Good to hear you laughing. As for Grady—"

"Like I said, I don't want to talk about him. He

also has a lot going on in his life. He doesn't need the complication of a pregnant woman."

"I know he cares for you," Lucy said. "You should tell him about the baby."

"I can't. I heard what he said, and I can't face any kind of rejection from him." The thought of his turning away from her thickened her throat.

"Are you leaving the ranch?"

"I can't yet. Cody has had too many disruptions in his little life."

"But if you and Grady—"

"I'll be fine," Chloe interrupted. "I just have to focus on my baby and do my job."

But even as she spoke those brave words, Chloe knew it would be much, much harder than that.

Chapter Fourteen

"Sorry I didn't come sooner." Grady settled himself in the chair beside his brother's bed, wincing as pain seized him, almost making him spill the cup of coffee he had bought for himself before coming up. Once again he felt sympathy for his father. How had he dealt with his pain day in and day out?

And, even harder, how had he faced their mother's rejection of him?

"It took me longer than usual to get here," Grady said. "Stubborn. Wanted to prove I could do this on my own, so I drove myself."

His leg still throbbed from being in one position so long. Thankfully his brother's truck had an automatic transmission. No clutch.

He had hoped to duck out without telling his grandmother he was going on his own, but she'd caught him before he left and handed him a thick, heavy envelope full of cash. Told him Chloe had received it and he had to give it over to the league. Thankfully she had said nothing about him driving to town.

But the envelope had bothered him. Chloe couldn't even be bothered to give it to him in person.

"We got stuck up at the ranch the past few days," he continued. "Freak snowstorm. Shut everything down."

He watched his brother closely, hoping, praying for even the slightest acknowledgment. The nurses had told him that Ben's eyes had opened again this morning, but now his brother lay perfectly still.

"Started doing some therapy, though I've skipped the past few days."

He had wondered how much good it would do. He could feel that he was stiffer today. But Chloe had been studiously avoiding him and hadn't said anything about therapy, and he wasn't about to ask, even though it was one of the reasons his grandmother had hired her.

"But the weather's turned, so that's good," he said to Ben as he shifted his position on the chair, trying to get comfortable. "Sun's shining and the snow is melting. It's a bluebird sky out there."

It was ironic that while storms blew around his

house, he had felt more serene and at peace than he had at most any other time in his life.

Because of Chloe.

Now that the sun was shining in a tranquil blue sky, his heart felt tossed and beaten and battered.

Because of Chloe. Who couldn't even be bothered to give him that lousy envelope in person.

"There's supposed to be another storm front blowing in. At least according to the forecaster. I sure hope not. The yard is still a sheet of ice, and I'm worried about the horses." He paused to take a sip of coffee, surprised at how much easier it was to talk to his brother now. Especially sitting here alone with no one waiting or hovering. Just him and Ben.

And because he was alone, he felt he had the space to tell his brother the things weighing like a rock on his mind since their last meeting. "I don't want to just talk about the weather," he said, looking down at his coffee cup, pulling together his apology. "I want to say again how sorry I am over how I left things between us before I left for this last tour. I'm sorry I was angry with you. You had a lot to deal with after I left. I had no right to be so self-righteous. I left you behind to deal with Dad and the ranch. I thought I was being all brave and heroic and honorable, but you were the brave and honorable one. You were the one who kept things going. I left you to do it alone and then judged how you did it. You're still my brother and I love you."

He stopped there, as if to let his confession settle somewhere in Ben's mind.

A cart pushed by a lab tech clattered past. Nurses at the station laughed at something.

Life flowed on regardless of the macro and micro tragedies of the world.

"I know that you're the easygoing one and I'm the worrier, so I should tell you that, as usual, I'm worried again. My leg doesn't seem to be getting any better and it hurts. A lot. Made me think of Dad and how hard it was to live with him."

Grady set his coffee aside, leaned forward in his chair. On a whim he took Ben's hand in his, surprised at how warm it felt. Still a horseman's hands with scars and rope burns and calluses.

"Remember how angry he got that time we took his truck out on the hayfield with some friends, burning doughnuts and acting like idiots? Fourteen years old and we had the world by the tail. Good thing Mom intervened or we would have been in worse trouble." He laughed lightly at the memory.

"I miss her, though I still get ticked at her for leaving Dad. I know he wasn't the easiest to live with, but I'm finally getting how hard it was for him. It's hard not to feel like less of a man when you can't do what you used to."

He stopped there, his own emotions suddenly in flux as he thought of Chloe. He felt his heart shift, shook his head and carried on.

"A couple of days ago I fell. It was bad enough to be sprawled out on the ice looking like some spavined mule, but it had to happen in front of Chloe. Yeah, the same Chloe who came here the last time. She's at the ranch now taking care of Cody and supposedly doing therapy with me, though she hasn't the past few days."

He stopped again, frustrated at how close his emotions were to the surface.

"I think she's given up because she saw what a hopeless case I am. Like Mom, after spending enough time with me she must realize I'm not getting better. That I'm this crippled man who has little to offer someone as wonderful as her." To his dismay, his voice broke.

"Listen to me," he said, adding a short laugh. "I've seen so much pain and sorrow overseas and here I am feeling sorry for myself over the loss of a woman. Trouble is this isn't just any woman. This is Chloe. Now, I know I've never been as good with girls as you have, so it might sound kind of pathetic to you, but I don't know what to do. I don't want to end up like Dad. I don't want her to be disappointed in me. I feel as if I've had something special, and now I don't know what happened to it."

He stopped there, feeling as if he had said too much. Opened himself too wide. Made himself too vulnerable.

Then he caught himself. What did it matter?

He bent his head, feeling as though he had hit the bottom.

And he knew what he had to do.

He held Ben's hand between his, bent his head and closed his eyes.

"I know I'm proud, Lord. I know that too often I want to do things on my own. But I'm facing big things that I can't fix. I can't push through with my will or my strength. You'd think I would have learned that overseas. I care for Chloe and I want what's best for her, but I can't make her love me. Take care of her. Watch over her. Be with my brother, as well."

He said amen, and stayed with his head bent a moment.

Then Ben's hand twitched in his. A slight movement, but a movement nonetheless.

He squeezed Ben's hand back and his heart dropped when Ben's hand moved again. Grady's eyes flew to Ben's face and to his amazement he saw Ben's eyelids drift upward. It was agonizing to watch. His lids fell shut again, but then once more, they slowly lifted. Ben blinked, then again and his head turned toward Grady. His hand twitched in Grady's again, then his fingers tightened for the briefest of moments.

Was that a smile?

Grady felt his heart quicken.

"Ben. Can you hear me? Squeeze my hand if you can hear me."

Ben's hand tightened briefly, then fell limp in his and his eyes closed again, and once again he lay still and unmoving.

Grady stood, watching, waiting for a few more minutes, but there was no more movement on Ben's part.

His heart filled with a mixture of expectation and disappointment.

What did he expect, that Ben would sit up and start talking?

Grady knew better than that, but even so it was a start. A tiny ray of blessing on a week that had been darkness and loneliness.

Fifteen minutes later he was on his way to a hastily called meeting of the Lone Star Cowboy League, his heart feeling just a bit lighter. As Ben's brother and a Stillwater, Grady had been elected to take his brother's place.

A number of vehicles were parked in front of the league building when he arrived. It looked as if most everyone was inside. With a grimace, Grady got out of the truck, pulled the hated crutch from behind the seat, locked his truck and hobbled up the snow-covered path to the door. Inside, he was greeted by the sound of angry voices, one of them Byron's.

Grady wasn't looking forward to this meeting. Though he had been back for a while now, he hadn't had much to do with the community as a whole, other than attending church on Sunday. The questions surrounding Cody's parenthood still seemed to cling to him, even though almost everyone should have known by now that the allegations were false. Vanessa was long gone and her accusations with her.

Nonetheless he took a deep breath, sent up a prayer for patience and walked into the building.

"Well, hello, Grady." Ingrid Edwards, the secretary of the league, sat at the desk by the entrance to the boardroom, her red hair hanging loose around her face. She pushed her glasses up her nose and got up, her hand out as if to help him. "I'm glad you're taking Ben's place."

"I hope I'm up to it," he said, taking a step away from her.

"So sad what happened to him." Ingrid gave him a shy smile. "And I was sorry to hear about your injury, too. That must have been so hard for you! Do you need a hand? I can hold your crutch while you take your coat off."

"I'm fine," Grady said, a little more gruffly

than he should have. Ingrid meant well; she just wasn't the most tactful person.

It was just that her view of him seemed to underline how he felt about himself. And how he was sure Chloe saw him.

Carson was standing in one corner of the room chatting with Lucy, who wore blue jeans and a faded denim shirt today, giving her a more approachable look than her uniform did. But this was negated by the frown beneath her blond fringe of hair.

Byron sat at the table, bent over some papers, glowering at whatever it was he was reading.

Carson looked up as Grady came in.

Was he imagining the look of pity on his face?

Grady knew he was being oversensitive.

"Well, the war hero is here," Byron said, getting up. "Mighty proud of you, son. You are a credit to our community."

Grady grew uncomfortable with the man's obvious bluster, and his discomfort only increased when Byron pulled a chair out for him.

"Here. Let me help you."

Why did everyone seem to think he was so helpless?

Maybe because he was, he thought, remembering his ungainly fall the other day.

"I can manage," Grady said, shaking off Byron's hand on his arm.

Then Lucy saw him and waved him over. "Grady. I need to talk to you."

"Excuse me," Grady said to Byron, who was frowning at him, obviously displeased that Grady had refused his help. But Grady wasn't about to try to soothe the man's ruffled feathers.

He made his way around the chairs to where Lucy stood, suspecting she wanted to discuss the thick envelope Chloe had left on the counter for him to pass on to Lucy. She was still avoiding him, and his grandmother was still trying to find out what had happened, but Grady didn't want to talk about it.

"Grady, good to see you here," Carson said, holding out his hand in greeting. "Though the reason you are here is less than ideal. How is Ben?"

Grady shook Carson's hand then shrugged. "Actually, there is some small improvement. Very small, but the doctor assured me he is moving in the right direction."

"We'll continue to pray for him," Carson said, giving Grady a tight smile. Then he turned back to Lucy. "I need to talk to Ingrid before we get started. Will you excuse me, please?"

Lucy nodded, waiting until Carson was out of earshot. She moved to the far corner of the room, turning so that her back was to the room. "Do you have the envelope?"

"Locked in my truck."

"Good. I'll have to present this to the meeting. Are you okay with that?"

"Yes. Why wouldn't I be?"

"It's just that the money came to Chloe while she was on your ranch. And Maddy, who also works at the Stillwater ranch, got some gifts, as well. Add that to the fact that you still haven't noticed anything missing..." She let the sentence hang as if expecting Grady to finish it.

He pushed down his anger at her unspoken suspicions, knowing she was simply doing her job. "I have no idea why we haven't been hit and people on our ranch have been getting things," he said. "Unless you suspect someone on the ranch."

Lucy blew out her breath, shooting another glance backward as if checking to see who might be listening in, but Byron had left the room as well, leaving the two of them alone.

"I don't suspect any of your employees, but you have to admit, it does seem odd that you haven't had anything stolen. I feel as if there's a connection, but I can't figure it out yet." She was silent, but Grady didn't add anything to her suspicions. He knew Josh, Emilio and Lucas couldn't possibly have anything to do with what had been going on. He trusted those men implicitly. As for the girls, he knew beyond a doubt they weren't involved.

"And how was your visit with Ben?" she asked.

"Like I said, very positive. I'm tempted to tell him a couple of lies, hoping he will try to wake up to set me straight."

Lucy gave him a sympathetic look. "But it's a good sign."

Grady nodded. "A very good sign."

"Chloe seems optimistic about your recovery, as well," Lucy said.

Even hearing her name hurt.

"We're not talking about...that."

Lucy bit her lip, looking back over her shoulder again at the empty room. She took a few steps closer and lowered her voice.

"So what happened with you and Chloe? I thought you two were getting somewhere?"

Grady pulled back, frowning at Lucy.

"Oh, don't get all 'mind your own business' on me," Lucy chided. "I talk to Chloe all the time. One minute she's all sappy and moony, the next she's weepy and miserable. What did you do to her?"

Grady could only stare. What was she talking about? Chloe miserable?

"What did *I* do to her?" He released a bitter snort. "She was the one who pulled away. Who cancelled my therapy sessions because she couldn't stand to be near me. Because she couldn't face the idea of maybe ending up with a man who wouldn't be able to do all the things he used to. Just like my mother couldn't." He didn't mean for that last comment to come out. He blamed it on his minitherapy session with his brother.

Lucy narrowed her eyes, watching him as if she couldn't understand what he was saying. "How do you figure that?"

Grady ground his teeth together, determined not to let Lucy and what she was talking about get to him.

"What makes you say that?" Lucy pressed. "She didn't say anything about your leg or disability. Just that she didn't think you would want to be with her because of her—" Lucy stopped there, holding up her hand, waving it as if to erase what she had just said.

"Because of her what?"

"Never mind. Talking too much. Blame it on being in civvies," she said, easing out a sigh.

"If this has something to do with what is happening between me and Chloe, you need to tell me."

"It's not my secret to tell," Lucy said, folding her arms over her chest, her feet planted slightly apart. Holding her ground.

"Secret?"

"You need to ask Chloe. Not me," Lucy said.

"But she's not talking to me." Grady clenched his fist, struggling to maintain his composure.

"Find a way. You're not the only one with pride, you know."

Grady couldn't help it. Hope fluttered deep in his soul, a fragile thing he hardly dared acknowledge but didn't want to ignore.

"Talk to her," Lucy said, adding a meaningful look. "Don't let her get away from you."

Grady held her gaze a moment, sensing that there had been more to the situation than his interpretation, and the flutter of hope grew. Just a bit.

"So why are we having this meeting, or are you two just going to sit in the corner sharing secrets?" Byron McKay called out, his loud voice breaking the silence that followed Lucy's comment. "Maybe you'd like to bring the rest of us into the loop. Tell us if you've solved any of the crimes. Maybe get that stolen Welcome to Little Horn sign back."

Lucy spun around, straightening her shoulders as if readying herself to face down Byron. "No secrets to share, Byron," she said as Carson, Tom Horn, Ingrid Edwards and other members of the Lone Star Cowboy League filed into the room. "As for the Welcome to Little Horn sign, I am looking into getting a new one made."

"Let's get going," Byron called out, looking

around as people settled into their seats. "Guess we'll have to find out just how incompetent our sheriff has been over the past week."

"That's out of order," Grady said.

Bryon rounded on him and Grady stared him down. Then Byron gave him what, for Byron, seemed to pass for an apologetic smile. "Right. Sorry."

Grady felt a small victory, but as he settled into the chair he had a hard time concentrating on the meeting. Over and over he thought of what Lucy had told him. Her truncated sentence about Chloe that raised more questions.

Because of her *what*?

He knew one thing: as soon as he got back to the ranch he was going to find out.

"What are your plans for this afternoon?" Mamie asked Chloe as she packaged up some cookies. "I was hoping to take these to Iva Donovan. See how she's doing."

"I thought I would take Cody out for a walk." Chloe finished giving him the last of his lunch and wiped the baby's mouth with a cloth. Cody tried to push away her hand, and in spite of the heaviness weighing on her heart she had to smile. "He's been cooped up quite a bit, and now that the sun is shining I'd like to get out, as well."

This way she would be out of the house when

Grady came back from his meeting with the league. She knew she couldn't avoid him forever and would have to resume his physical therapy sessions soon, but she needed a few days to settle herself in this hard place.

Chloe wiped Cody's hands and got up to bring his bowl to the sink. She returned to the high chair and unbuckled his harness, then picked him up. After she settled him on her hip, she cuddled him close, pressing a kiss to his head. Tears pricked her eyelids. The past few days it was as if her pregnancy was making her feel even more maternal and fragile.

"Honey, is everything okay?"

Mamie's quiet voice and gentle hand on her shoulder didn't help Chloe's precarious emotions.

She swallowed the knot in her throat and struggled to regain her composure.

"Yes, everything is fine."

But her assertion didn't come out as strongly as she had hoped, and her voice trembled on the last word.

"I don't think it is at all," Mamie said, slipping her arm around Chloe's waist and steering her gently toward the living room. "In fact, I think we need to talk."

Her words created an ominous feeling inside. Did Mamie know about her pregnancy? Was she about to get fired for misleading her? Where would she go now? What would she do?

Just wait. Don't borrow trouble.

Chloe pulled in a long, slow breath and sat down, holding Cody a little tighter than necessary. He wiggled as though he wanted to leave, so she set him on the floor.

"He just keeps getting bigger and bigger," Mamie said as she sat down on the couch beside Chloe. They watched him crawl away, then sit up, smiling proudly at his achievement.

Then Mamie turned to Chloe, took her hand.

Chloe swallowed, and swallowed again, trying to stifle the fear clawing up her throat.

"I promised myself I would never be a meddling grandma," Mamie said, giving Chloe's hand a gentle squeeze. "But I'm going to now. I noticed that you and Grady seemed to enjoy each other's company. I thought you were attracted to him and vice versa. In fact, I was kind of thinking the way things were going that you and him were building a relationship. But now…" She shrugged, waited as if hoping Chloe would fill in the blanks, but Chloe, not trusting herself to speak, said nothing.

"I know that working here isn't the same as working in the hospital," Mamie said with a sense of finality. "And I think you know that I asked you to come for a bunch of reasons and not just because I needed help with Cody. I could have asked any number of people to help me. And yes, I was hoping you would be able to convince Grady that he needed to do therapy, but I'm sure I could have done that myself."

Mamie gave her a rueful smile. "I may as well tell the truth. I was hoping that you and Grady would get together. I know you used to like him in high school, and I'm positive he had a thing for you until that Vanessa girl got her claws in him." This was followed by another long-suffering sigh. "And then, for a while, it seemed that you two found each other. That you were, well, falling in love. But now you two can't even spend time together in the same room. So I'm coming right out and asking...what happened?"

Chloe looked down at their joined hands, so close to the growing swell of her stomach. Talking about Grady still hurt too much. She didn't trust herself to be objective. Not to cry.

If she told Mamie about the baby, which would be hard enough, she might be distracted enough not to ask her any more painful questions about Grady.

Sending up a prayer for strength, she took a breath and held Mamie's questioning gaze.

"I'm pregnant."

"I know."

Chloe could only stare. Mamie's blunt response was not what she had expected at all.

"How did you know?" she asked when the shock wore off.

Mamie shrugged. "I didn't know for sure. I just guessed, but I guess I know for sure now." She gave Chloe's hand a comforting squeeze. "Don't worry. I haven't told anyone. And it doesn't matter. I'm thinking that your ex-husband is the father?"

"Jeremy. Yes. I got pregnant and he didn't want a baby. Didn't take him long to get rid of me thanks to his close friendship with a judge."

"It's okay, sweetie. You don't have to explain."

"But I feel as if I do. I took this job under false pretenses."

"I'm thinking Grady doesn't know?"

Chloe shook her head, the last words that he'd spoken to her still ringing in her mind.

"Why haven't you told him? I know you care for him."

Chloe heard the faint reprimand in Mamie's voice and tried not to feel defensive. "I was afraid. Everything happened so quickly and it was so wonderful." She looked up at Grady's grand-mother, praying she would understand. "You are right when you say I've cared for Grady a long time. We were on our way to building a relation-ship and everything was working out so well. I was so happy."

"What happened?"

Chloe bit her lip, casting through her mind for the right words.

"We were talking about Cody and he said that he was thankful that Cody wasn't his because he didn't…didn't want to start a relationship with the responsibility of a child. He said that was heavy stuff. And at that moment I knew I couldn't tell him about my baby."

Mamie's silence underlined Chloe's insecurities.

"He kept telling me how much he appreciated my honesty and innocence," she continued. "And here I am, not only divorced, but pregnant by the man I just divorced. It just makes me feel…unworthy."

"Oh, child, never think that," Mamie hastily said, giving Chloe a hug. Then she framed Chloe's face with her hands, shaking her head as if in disbelief. "You are indeed a pure and innocent person. You were trying to stay true to your vows, and that is already beyond admirable. That you got pregnant doing so was not your fault."

"Thank you for that," Chloe said, catching Mamie by the wrists, smiling at her. "But it doesn't negate the fact that Grady doesn't think he can take on a child."

"You don't know that for sure. You don't know exactly what he was referring to. What he meant. I still think you should tell him."

"For what purpose? I doubt he will change how he feels about taking on the responsibility."

Mamie said nothing to that, which only underlined what Chloe knew she had to do.

"I know you hired me to work with Grady, but I don't know if I can do that anymore." Chloe bit her lip, looking over at Cody, who was gumming on a small teddy bear, looking up at them, his eyes sparkling. Her heart lurched in her chest. "I don't want to do this to Cody, and if you want, I will stay to take care of him—"

"Honey, don't make any decisions right away," Mamie said. "You have a home here as long as you need it."

"I also have a furnished apartment in town," Chloe said with a forced laugh.

"That's not a home."

Chloe agreed, but she couldn't see that she had any choice.

"You know you can stay here as long as you need to," Mamie said.

"Thank you," Chloe said.

"And I think you should talk to Grady. You need to tell him about your baby and let him decide how he feels about it."

"But he said—"

"I know what he said, but that was about Cody. For all you know, he might have felt guilty because he thought he couldn't take care of him given his injury." Mamie was quiet a moment. "I don't know if you know the full history of Grady and his parents."

"All I know is that his parents got divorced when Grady was in junior high."

"Did you know why?"

"I was young then. I can't remember." Plus she'd had had her own drama going on in her home. That had been about the time Etta and Vanessa had come into Chloe's life.

Mamie pulled in a slow breath. "I think what happened with my son and his wife has had an impact on both boys, and not for the better. My son, Reuben, had an accident a couple of years before the divorce. He was feeding cows and a bale fell on him and injured his back. After that he was in constant pain and couldn't do as much as he used to. He wasn't the easiest man to live with before, and he became much more difficult after that. Shirley couldn't handle living with him. Two years after the accident, she left him.

"Grady was angry and humiliated, and as soon as he could, he joined the army. I always thought he figured it was a way of redeeming the family name. Grady and his father were always close, and after he left, Reuben became even more bitter. While Grady could always get along with him, Ben couldn't. Which caused problems in Ben's life." Mamie was silent a moment. Then she gave Chloe a gentle smile. "I may be wrong, but when Grady got injured I wonder if, on some level, he didn't think a woman would want him the way he was. His mother couldn't live with an injured man. Maybe no woman could live with him."

Chloe let Mamie's words roll over in her mind as she examined them. She thought of how he initially had resisted her help. She knew he was proud and stubborn; what Mamie had told her gave another layer to his personality.

Then she felt a movement in her abdomen and she felt herself drawn back to another reality. Her own situation. And what she brought to any relationship she and Grady might have.

Another man's child. Could he handle that?

She wasn't sure she wanted to find out. She wasn't sure she could face rejection again.

"You and Grady were meant to be together," Mamie said, squeezing Chloe's hand. "I've prayed so often that Grady would find someone. When you came into his life, I thought those prayers were answered. I don't like to think God was toying with me."

Chloe wasn't sure what to say to that. She knew that relationships were difficult.

"You think about what I said," Mamie urged. "Don't give up on Grady yet. He's a good man, and in spite of what you may think, you're a good woman. Grady is a proud person, but part of me thinks that maybe you have your share of pride, as well."

Chloe felt taken aback by her comment, then, as she thought about it, she understood what Mamie was saying. "I might. It hasn't been easy for me, either, knowing that my father couldn't seem to keep his ranch together. And then me getting a divorce and losing my job." She sighed, trying not to let the despair that hung over her like a cloud darken her perspective. "Maybe I tried to protect myself, as well."

"Of course you have," Mamie said, giving her hands a gentle shake. "But these events are not what define you. These are things that happened to you. These things are not you. You have much to give my grandson. I want you to think about that, as well. And I want you to know that you can trust him with your heart and with that baby you're carrying."

Chloe gave her a half smile. "Thanks for the encouragement." She gave into an impulse and brushed a light kiss over Mamie's cheek. "Thank you for everything."

She got up, picked up Cody and brought him to the porch to get him ready. She needed to get outside and get some fresh air.

Then she needed to figure out what her next step was.

Chapter Fifteen

Grady got out of Ben's truck, then ducked his head against the snow that had started up again just as he'd pulled into the yard. The meeting had dragged on far longer than it had needed to. After what Lucy had hinted at, he'd wanted to leave right away and return to the ranch to talk to Chloe.

But Byron had kept saying how Lucy was dragging her heels and had grilled Grady on the background of the people working at Stillwater Ranch. He had dropped many a broad hint about the lack of thefts from their ranch. Grady had had a hard time not losing his patience. It was only because Lucy had voiced the same concerns that he'd given Byron the information he had. But it bothered him that people were suspecting employees he had known for so many years. People his brother trusted implicitly.

Then the money had brought out another round of protests from Lenora Woods, who'd seemed to think that if anyone needed help it was her, not some single girl who could take care of herself. Byron kept calling for Lucy's resignation. It was tiring and Grady had forgotten what a blowhard Byron could be.

Carson had managed to rein Byron in and they'd finally gotten through the agenda. But throughout the meeting Grady had kept thinking about what Lucy had said.

He made his way into the house, torn between hurrying and making sure he didn't fall again. His leg was getting sore again, but he didn't want to dwell on that. He needed to find Chloe. To figure out what Lucy was talking about.

Don't let her get away from you.

You're not the only one with pride.

Lucy's words had spun around his head all the way home. The smile she'd given him had ignited a tiny spark of hope.

Once inside he shucked his coat, inhaling the scent of cookies, his growling stomach reminding him he hadn't eaten anything since breakfast. He followed his nose to the kitchen, hoping that Chloe would be there. As he wolfed down a couple of cookies, he listened. But the house was silent.

He heard a vehicle pull up and he hurried to the door just as his grandmother came inside.

"Do you know where Chloe and Cody are?" Grady asked.

His grandmother shook her head as she unwound a thick scarf from around her neck, stamping off the snow from her boots. "No. I've been gone for an hour or so. She said she was taking Cody for a walk. She left the same time I did. She isn't back yet?" Mamie's voice took on an edge that added to Grady's concern.

"No. She's not." Grady pulled back, analyzing. Breaking things down. "I'll go check at the barns. She might be there."

He slipped his coat back on, dropped his hat on his head and grabbed his gloves.

"Do you want me to come?" his grandmother asked, worry lacing her voice.

"No. I'm sure it's fine," Grady said, not wanting to add to her concern. *One step at a time*, he told himself. *First plan A. Check the barn.*

He tugged on his gloves, wrapping a scarf around his neck to cut the wind that he heard picking up.

He walked carefully across the yard to the barn, ducking his head against the icy wind. As the snow hit his cheeks he hoped they weren't in for another storm.

But all was quiet in the barn. Just to make

sure, he hurried down the alley. Sweetpea whinnied at him as he went past. Babe and Shiloh just watched him go.

Grady's heart turned in his chest. Chloe and Cody weren't here. They weren't in the house. Then, where would they have gone for so long? He tried to call her on her cell phone but didn't receive an answer. He guessed she was in a place with poor reception or her battery was dead. Either way, he had no idea where she could be.

He tried to settle his growing concern. Think. Analyze.

He remembered his grandmother saying the last time Chloe had taken Cody out it was for a ride in his sled toward the south ridge. But how far had they gone? He didn't dare walk on this ice.

No one was around to help and his grandmother couldn't do anything. He had to go find her, but how?

He'd have to saddle up one of the horses.

He found a halter and headed out into the pasture. Thankfully the horses had just been fed and were standing around the hay bale that one of the hands had given them. It took some awkward maneuvering, but he finally caught Apollo, one of the quieter horses, and led him back to the barn where the tack room was located. Once inside, he faced another obstacle trying to saddle up the horse on his own. He hadn't done it since he'd been back and he knew he was wasting valuable time trying to manage. So he swallowed his pride and hurried to the house as quickly as he dared.

His leg was aching by the time he got back to the house.

"Grandma! I need your help," he called out, sticking his head in the door.

"I'm right here." She appeared immediately. "What do you need?"

"Help with the horse. I'm going out to find Chloe and Cody."

Mamie grabbed her coat and shoved her feet into her boots, then headed out.

But she was faster than he was and while he tried to keep up, he was afraid of falling and injuring himself. He would be no good to Chloe if he was flat on his back.

Mamie looked behind her then, came back, tucked her shoulder under his arm and helped him to the barn. Once again he had to fight down his innate sense of independence, thankful that it helped him move just a bit faster.

He and Mamie got Apollo saddled up in record time. He kept telling himself not to panic. Chloe had probably just gone farther than usual and once the wind started up, decided to head back. She wasn't reckless. She was careful.

She was alone.

"You haven't lost your touch," Grady said as

he tightened up the cinch, making sure all was snug and secure.

"Like riding a bike." Mamie took the horse's bridle and started leading him away.

"Where are you going?" Grady asked, grabbing his crutch and stumbling along behind her.

"You can't climb up on that horse on your own," Grandma said, leading him to the box they had used when Grady and Ben were youngsters.

Grady almost balked, but he couldn't get all puffed up now. Too much was at stake.

So he took the steps one at a time, then climbed on the horse. Without a word Mamie carefully lifted his injured leg and slipped his foot into the stirrup, then she slipped the reins over Apollo's head and handed them to Grady.

"Ride safe," she said. "Please find them. I'll be praying for you."

"While you're praying, call Clint Daniels and Finn. We could use their expertise. And call Emilio and a couple of the other boys, as well."

She nodded as she walked ahead of him to the entrance of the barn. She opened the door and he rode out into the blowing snow.

Chloe trudged along the packed trail she had walked along down in the draw, pulling Cody on the sled, her mind weighing and measuring what Mamie had told her.

Part of her didn't dare cling to the hope Mamie's words had kindled. Her sense of self-preservation had been honed while living with Jeremy and afterward.

But the part of her that had always yearned for Grady, that had cherished every moment they spent together the past few weeks, greedily latched on to the tiniest crumbs.

"What do you think, Cody?" she asked the little boy, who was sitting like a little mummy on the sled behind her. "Do you think I should tell Grady about my baby? Do you think I should take that chance?"

Cody just sat there grinning at her, his cheeks rosy and his eyes bright.

"You are so adorable," she said, laughing in spite of herself. "You don't even care that your daddy is in a coma and you have no clue who your momma is, do you? As long as you're taken care of it doesn't matter. Maybe I need to be more like you. Just trust that God will take care of me, whatever shape that takes."

Cody waved his mittened hands as if agreeing with her, barely able to move in the restrictive snowsuit, his stocking cap shifting down and covering his eyes. Chloe stopped and gently pushed it back up, squatting down and checking if he was warm enough.

"I just wish I knew what to do," she said,

brushing some snow off his snowsuit. "Mamie said I could trust Grady, but part of me wants to let him remember me as this supposedly pure and innocent person."

He would find out the truth soon enough, but by that time she probably would be gone.

She stood and the wind, gusting now, pulled her scarf away from her neck. It seemed the storm was picking up. Down in the draw the sound was muffled, but she knew she would have to go up that hill sooner or later.

Today she had gone farther than she usually did, and now it sounded as if the bad weather they had predicted for tomorrow was coming sooner than expected. She started looking for the path up the hill. Another blast of wind tossed snow at her and she wrapped her scarf closer around her, now feeling irresponsible for taking Cody so far.

She stepped up her pace and looked around to make sure Cody was okay. Then she turned just as she hit an icy patch. Her feet slipped and she tried to catch her balance. Her foot hit a root, rolled onto its side, and she collapsed into the snow in an ungainly heap. Thankfully she kept hold of the rope pulling Cody's sled, but as she tried to get up, searing pain shot through her ankle and up into her leg.

Chloe's heart sank as she dropped into the snow again, riding out the wave of pain.

She sucked in a breath, then another as it subsided into a dull, steady throb.

Wrenched for sure, maybe sprained.

She had a good fifteen-minute walk ahead of her, and she had to get up to the top of the hill yet.

Dread clutched her as another gust of icy wind howled down the gully. On top she and Cody would be out in the open, but she couldn't stay here. If someone went out looking for her, they wouldn't find her.

"Stupid, stupid," she muttered, feeling silly, irresponsible and frightened.

"We're going to be okay," Chloe murmured, as much to herself as to the little boy in the sled. "We'll be okay."

Please, Lord, help me be okay. Help me and Cody to make it out of here. Give me strength to get us home.

She tried not to let desperation pull her down as the wind whistled around her. She pulled her scarf off and wrapped it around the baby's face for extra protection against the wind. All she could see were his bright eyes and, thankfully, he seemed fine. She glanced around, looking for a stick she could use to walk with.

There. To her left. A branch lay half-covered in snow. She clenched her teeth against a wave of pain shooting up from her ankle as she took another hesitant step toward it, then a hop, then a step. Each movement made it feel as if glass was imbedded in her leg. After what seemed like ages, she made it to where the branch was. She pulled it loose from the snow, whimpering as she lost her balance and landed on her sore ankle. She had to think of Grady with each wave of pain, knowing that he dealt with this all the time, surprised it didn't make him grumpy or miserable.

Looping the rope from the sled around one arm, Chloe used the branch to make her clumsy way up the hill. Each time she slipped, the weight of the sled pulled her back. Slowly, slowly she made her way up, dragging the sled behind her. She stopped a couple of times to make sure Cody wasn't toppling off, but he was okay.

After what seemed like hours, she made it to the top of the hill. She sat down, rested a moment, thankful for one small victory. In spite of the chilly wind and biting snow, she was sweating with exertion. Not good, she thought, as she was now exposed and so was Cody.

But he was covered and she knew she couldn't get to the ranch carrying him. She would just have to keep going. She pulled her cell phone out of her pocket and felt another stab of dismay. No service.

Help me, Lord, she prayed, shoving her phone back in her pocket. She got up, grabbed her stick and started hobbling toward the ranch, her head down against the slanting snow. All she could do was take one step. Then another.

And keep praying.

Chapter Sixteen

Grady squinted into the blowing snow, wishing he could see better. The track he had been following was getting snowed in but so far it looked as if Chloe had stayed on this trail. Hopefully she hadn't veered off. The sun was going down. In an hour or so it would be dark.

And then what?

He didn't want to think about that. All he could think about was Chloe and Cody and getting to them and returning them home.

He leaned forward, ignoring the pain in his leg as minor compared to the fear that gripped his heart. It was getting colder. How long would Chloe and Cody last in this weather if he didn't find them?

As he rode, he thought of other missions he'd been on that didn't end well. He pushed those thoughts back. He couldn't think of that. He reminded himself that each time he went out it was with success in mind.

Please, Lord...

His prayer was simple, a cry from his heart.

He didn't know why Chloe had pulled herself back from him. Didn't know why she was avoiding him.

He should have fought for her.

Don't let her get away from you.

Lucy's words spurred him on and he nudged Apollo in the ribs, ignoring the pain in his leg.

Cowboy up, his father had always told Grady and Ben when things got tough and they wanted to quit. Those words were exactly appropriate now.

Please, Lord...

His horse lifted his head, as if sensing something. Grady peered through the now-driving snow, seeing nothing. But if there was one thing he had learned when riding horses in uncertain situations: trust the horse. Pay attention to its body language.

Apollo's ears pricked forward and he slowed. A horse's first reflex was flight so it made sense that, if he saw something, he would slow down. The horse whinnied softly and then he heard a yell.

"Help! Please, help!"

Chloe.

Thank You, Lord.

Grady nudged his horse in the ribs, leaning to one side, favoring his good leg as he tried to look through the driving snow. "Chloe? Where are you?" He still couldn't see her.

"I'm here."

He tried to follow her voice then saw a darker form that eventually took shape. Chloe, leaning against a tree, Cody in the sled behind her.

"Please, help us."

"I'm here," Grady said. "I'm here."

He rode closer and relief spread like warm honey through his veins when he saw Cody waving his arms. Chloe stood, then faltered.

"Are you okay?"

"I sprained my ankle," she said, pain lacing her voice. "Cody's okay, though."

Grady looked from Cody to her, thinking.

"Do you think you can get on the horse?"

"Just get Cody home, I'll get there eventually."

"Not a chance. Hand him to me," Grady said, not daring to get off the horse himself. He knew he couldn't get back on the horse or make his way back without his crutch. "I want you to try to climb on."

Chloe simply nodded, and pulled the sled closer, tugged her mittens off and unbuckling the strap that held the baby in. It took a few moments longer than normal, then she handed Cody up to him.

Grady shifted Cody to one arm and held out his hand to her and kicked his one foot out of the stirrup. "This will hurt, no matter which foot you use, but you can do it. Put your foot in the stirrup, hang on to the horn of the saddle and climb on."

She bit her lip but then nodded, clearly not seeing another way around this predicament. Grady shifted himself as far back in the saddle as he could. She wouldn't be able to swing her leg around, which meant he had to let go of the reins as she clambered on. Hopefully Apollo would behave and not try anything funny.

It took a couple of tries, but finally Chloe was settled in front of him on the saddle, Cody in her arms. She had the presence of mind to lean forward and grab the reins. Grady reached around her and took them in his hands, thankful that the wind was now in their back. As Apollo started walking it felt as if the storm had eased off.

"How's your ankle?" Grady asked, shifting so there was enough room, wincing even as he did so.

"It hurts. How's your leg?"

"It hurts, too."

"Is Cody okay?"

"His hands are toasty warm and so is his head. He's fine."

They rode in silence for a while. The wind that had tossed snow at him and whistled around his ears seemed quieter now that it was behind them. The forest looked peaceful with the snow falling down around them.

Chloe shifted, tossing a look over her shoulder. "Thanks for coming to get me. I shouldn't have gone out. It was risky."

"You didn't know the storm was coming as soon as it did. And you didn't know you would sprain your ankle." He held the reins in one hand as he lifted the collar of his coat, protecting his neck from the snow. "It wasn't your fault."

Chloe said nothing and the questions haunting him circled his brain like ravens.

Ask her why she avoided you. Ask her if your disability is a problem.

But asking the question would make him vulnerable, and he thought of his father and what he went through after his injury. How his mother hadn't been able to handle it. Couldn't deal.

But was Chloe the same?

Somehow, even as he examined the question, he sensed he was giving her short shrift. And having Chloe in his arms felt so good, so right. It was such a stark reminder of what he had been missing. And now that they were alone, he realized how foolish it was to go on acting as if nothing had happened.

Don't let her get away from you.

He had to know.

"Why did you—"

"I need to tell you—"

They both spoke at once, then stopped.

Grady laughed lightly, the awkwardness plaguing both of them apparent in how Chloe hunched her shoulders, how stiffly he held the reins.

He loosened his grip, which meant he was holding Chloe even closer. He could feel her relax against him. He felt a renewed surge of hope.

"What happened, Chloe?" he asked, putting himself out there, making himself vulnerable. "When you turned away from me after we spent that afternoon in the barn. Was it because I fell? Because you were reminded of how less of a man I am?

"What are you talking about?" The question burst out of Chloe. "Is that what you think? That's crazy. Why would you think that?" Her back stiffened as if underlining her reaction to his questions. He wished he could see her face, but he could only keep talking, hoping she understood what he was saying.

"I'm sorry, but it's just that my mother left my father after his accident. She couldn't live with him. Vanessa kept harping how my disability was a problem she was willing to overlook. Guess I'm just a bit sensitive."

"You're not…not less of a man. That's a ridiculous thing to think. I don't know why you would even entertain the idea that I'm that…shallow, unfeeling, and I don't appreciate being compared to Vanessa."

Her chagrin both surprised him and fanned the tiny spark of hope Lucy's comments had created.

"I wasn't comparing, just thinking—"

"That's good, because your mom was wrong to leave, and I'm nothing like Vanessa. I care about you, a lot, and I thought I was…"

"Was what?" he prompted.

But she said nothing. Yet he felt as if she had been on the verge of saying something he wanted to hear.

"I'm sorry," he said, still trying to absorb this angry version of Chloe. "I just thought…after I fell on the ice, that's when you pulled away. If it wasn't what I thought it was, then why?"

She looked down, fussing with Cody's stocking cap, shifting him on her lap, as if putting off her reply. His horse plodded along, picking his way over the icy patches, and Grady hoped and prayed he wouldn't stumble. He was carrying a precarious load.

"Why then?" he urged, sensing that something else was coming. He hoped he was ready.

She pulled in a breath, her shoulders tensing.

"I'm pregnant," she said.

"What?"

"I'm pregnant. Jeremy is the father."

Grady tried to absorb this information, tried to figure out where to put it in his mind.

"So when is the baby due?"

"I'm not quite five months. Our marriage was stumbling along," she said, her voice quiet as if she hardly dared let the information leave her. "But I had made promises and wanted to be faithful. Then I got pregnant. Jeremy never wanted children. He got angry and filed for divorce. He had a judge who was a good friend and managed to get it done extraquick. After that he disappeared. I haven't been able to track him down to discuss child support. I was on my own." Grady had to bend closer to Chloe to hear what she was saying, and each word was like a small blow. Unsettling and surprising at the same time.

"He said he didn't want to have anything to do with the baby. That's why he wanted the divorce. So when you said what you did about Cody…I thought…I thought you would feel the same way, especially because this baby isn't yours the same way Cody isn't."

Her voice broke on the last words and Grady's heart plunged. He felt so bad for her obvious distress and he wrapped one arm more tightly around her, trying to find the right words to say what was spinning through his mind. Yes, he was confused and yes, this was a shock, but for her to think he wouldn't want to have anything to do with her baby?

Chloe took in a shaky breath, which made him feel even worse for her. She was clearly upset, and that bothered him even more than it did to find out she was pregnant.

"Why would you think I would feel the same way that Jeremy did?"

"Because of what you said about Cody. Just before you fell. But it was what you said that made me pull away from you. Not you falling."

Grady skipped back, trying to remember. "I'm sorry. I can't remember."

"You said…you said that you didn't want to think of starting a relationship with the responsibility of a child. You said that was heavy."

"I said that? About Cody?" Grady tried to catch up as he realized what she was referring to.

She nodded, reaching up to swipe at her cheeks with a gloved hand.

Grady's heart melted at the thought of her tears and he cradled her even closer. He wished he could see her face. Wished he could tip her chin up to look into her eyes, wished she could see the sincerity in his own. "What I said was referring to the fact that Cody had a mother we knew nothing about. That he was dumped on my grandmother's doorstep without any notice. It was the mess that came with it. Vanessa, my brother in a coma. I was referring to that. The responsibility of that. The heaviness of all that." He struggled, wishing, hoping he was making himself clear. Because he felt as if he and Chloe were balancing on the edge of something large and life changing, and the right or wrong words could send him in either direction. And he knew he couldn't hold back any longer.

He leaned closer, pressing his cheek to hers. "I don't know if you're ready to hear this or not, but I have to tell you how much I care about you. I've been miserable the past few days, and it isn't just because my leg's been bugging me. My heart's been bugging me more. I missed you and I hope you missed me." He took in a breath, sent up a prayer, then said, "I love you. I want you in my life no matter what happens."

In spite of the movement of the horse, Chloe suddenly became perfectly still. He heard her draw in a shaky breath and he wondered if he had spoken too soon. He shifted a bit to try to see her, but her face, this close in his peripheral vision, was a blur. He couldn't read her expression or guess what she was thinking.

"Oh, Grady," she whispered, bringing one gloved hand up to his face. "I can't believe I'm hearing this. It's so much." She released a light laugh and he could feel her cheek lift in a smile.

"I have to say I've been miserable without you, as well. I missed you so much." She pulled in another breath. "And I love you, too."

Grady's heart felt as if it was going to explode out of his chest. At the same time he felt as if a burdensome, uncomfortable pack had slipped off his back leaving him feel weightless. Free.

"You love me?" He could hardly believe it.

"I love you."

He wanted to kiss her. But for now he had to content himself with holding her tight with one arm, his cheek pressed to hers, his heart beating against her back.

I love her.

She loves me.

Chloe wanted to cry, to laugh, to turn and give Grady a hug, but all she could do was press her hand to his cheek, hoping he could feel how her heart sang with a joy she couldn't find words for.

"I shouldn't have assumed" was all she could say. "I should have stayed and talked to you, but I was so afraid."

"So was I," he said. Then he pressed a kiss to her cheek.

She lay her head back against him, still holding Cody who, thankfully, sat quietly in her lap. She was about to say something more when a voice called out from the darkness.

"Grady? Is that you?"

Chloe saw a shadowy figure on horseback coming toward them through the falling snow.

"I just got here. All set to head out and rescue you," Emilio said as he came nearer, sounding disappointed. "Clint is on his way, as well."

"How far is the ranch?" Chloe asked, squinting through the snow and gathering dusk.

"Only a couple hundred yards ahead," Emilio said. "You all okay?"

"We're all fine," Grady said.

"Mamie will be glad to see you. Josh had to hold her back from saddling up and heading out herself," Emilio said as he turned his horse around, waiting for them to catch up. He glanced down at Cody. "You look overburdened there. You want me to take him?"

"It might be more comfortable for him." Chloe's one arm was growing tired, holding him up and away from the saddle horn. There was only so much room.

Emilio moved his horse closer and, reaching over, took Cody from her. "Hey, little guy," Emilio said, settling the baby in front of him. "You've had an adventure." Emilio looked at Grady. "I'll just bring him to the ranch right away. Let Mamie know you two are okay."

"That'd be good," Grady said, his voice a rumble against her back. "We'll be along shortly. I don't want to rush Apollo."

"Sure thing." Emilio tugged down his hat, hunched his shoulders against the wind and set out back to the ranch.

Chloe couldn't think of what to say as Emilio disappeared into the snow. Part of her wanted to stop right here and now, but her feet were getting cold, her hands were icy and her ankle was throbbing.

What a time to have the man you love express his own love for you.

"We should be there in a couple of minutes," Grady said, wrapping his one arm around her middle, pulling her tightly back against him.

It was less than that by the time they got to the yard. The glow of the house lights was inviting and Emilio's horse was tied up close to the house. Clearly Mamie had already heard the news about their safety and Cody was in good hands.

Grady steered the horse toward the barn. He stopped by the large rolling door and dismounted slowly. Chloe could see he was stiff and sore and struggled with her guilt. She should have been working with him. It was what she had been hired for.

I was going to, she reminded herself as Grady led the horse into the warm, softly lit barn. *Eventually.*

He brought the horse to the nearest stall and

tied him up. His crutch was still leaning against a wall. He grabbed it, then he walked to Chloe's side and held his arms up to help her.

She managed to put her weight on her good leg and slowly dismount, Grady supporting her. She got down, but as soon as she put even the smallest amount of weight on her foot, she stumbled.

Grady caught her, wavering, as well.

They stood, leaning against each other.

Grady laughed. "I guess you can identify with me right now."

"I can," she agreed, finding her balance again. She still clung to him, but that was as much for emotional support as physical.

"And I guess right now we need each other. To support each other."

"In more ways than one," she said, looking up at him, tugging off her gloves. Though her fingers were chilled, she cupped his dear face in her hands, the stubble on his chin only making him more rugged and appealing.

Then he did what she had been longing for him to do. He bent his head, pulled her close and kissed her.

She sighed as he pulled away, her heart full.

"Is this real?" she asked, trying to absorb the wonder of it all.

"I hope so," Grady said. He shifted his weight, winced and nodded. "Yup. It's real."

Chloe laughed then grew serious as she looked up at him, asking the question that she both dreaded and yet knew needed to be dealt with. "And my baby?"

Grady put his hand on the tiny swell of her stomach that seemed to have come out in only the past few days, his hand warm, comforting.

"I love you," he said. "I love you so much. And I know I will love this baby, because he or she is a part of you. I won't lie that I'm nervous about it. I think I said what I did about Cody because I'm not sure what kind of father I could be. But this baby, this child, we would be taking care of together. And I know you'll be an amazing mother and will help me learn to be an amazing father. We'll be doing this together. I don't know if I'll be able to be the active father I had always thought I could be—"

Chloe put her finger on his lips. "I love you just the way you are. You are the best man I know. You are everything I want, and you will be everything this baby and any baby we have together needs." She put her weight on one foot, then stretched up to kiss him, underlining her vow.

He smiled back at her then gave her another hug. "I'm so thankful for you. And I pray that God will bless us and our life together." Then he pulled back. "And now we should make our way back to the house to get Emilio to take care of this horse and to tell Mamie. I'm sure she's wondering what's happening."

"I have a feeling she knows exactly what is happening," Chloe said with a grin. "But I'm sure she wants to hear for herself."

"Then, let's go," Grady said. "Let's go back to the house. Let's go back home."

And leaning on each other, supporting one another, they did exactly that.

* * * * *

If you liked this
LONE STAR COWBOY LEAGUE *novel,*
watch for the next book,
A DADDY FOR HER TRIPLETS,
by Deb Kastner, available February 2016.

And don't miss a single story in the
LONE STAR COWBOY LEAGUE *miniseries:*

Book #1: A REUNION FOR THE RANCHER
by Brenda Minton

Book #2: A DOCTOR FOR THE NANNY
by Leigh Bale

Book #3: A RANGER FOR THE HOLIDAYS
by Allie Pleiter

Book #4: A FAMILY FOR THE SOLDIER
by Carolyne Aarsen

Book #5: A DADDY FOR HER TRIPLETS
by Deb Kastner

Book #6: A BABY FOR THE RANCHER
by Margaret Daley

Dear Reader,

Chloe has a secret and she is ashamed of it. Grady has a disability and he, too, is ashamed of it. Both have valid reasons to be concerned about how they will be viewed by the other. But life and relationships are all about being vulnerable to each other. And being vulnerable requires trust, as does any relationship. I know I have a hard time letting myself be vulnerable and letting people see my insecurities, but I have found when I do this within the bounds of a loving relationship, that relationship is enhanced and deepened.

I hope that you enjoyed reading Chloe and Grady's story and that you will read the rest of the books in the Lone Star Cowboy League series to solve the mystery of the thefts and baby Cody!

Blessings,

Carolyne Aarsen

PS: I love to hear from readers. Drop me a line at caarsen@xplornet.com. You can also stop by my website at www.carolyneaarsen.com and sign up for my newsletter to stay informed of new releases.

LARGER-PRINT BOOKS!

GET 2 FREE
LARGER-PRINT NOVELS
PLUS 2 FREE
MYSTERY GIFTS

Love Inspired®
SUSPENSE
RIVETING INSPIRATIONAL ROMANCE

Larger-print novels are now available...

LISLP15

REQUEST YOUR FREE BOOKS!
2 FREE WHOLESOME ROMANCE NOVELS
IN LARGER PRINT
PLUS 2
FREE
MYSTERY GIFTS

★ ★ ★ ★ ★ ★ ★ ★ ★ ★ ★ ★ ★ ★ ★ ★ ★ ★ ★ ★

HEARTWARMING™

❀ ❀ ❀ ❀ ❀ ❀ ❀ ❀ ❀ ❀ ❀ ❀ ❀ ❀ ❀ ❀ ❀ ❀ ❀ ❀

Wholesome, tender romances

YES! Please send me 2 FREE Harlequin® Heartwarming Larger-Print novels and my 2 FREE mystery gifts (gifts worth about $10). After receiving them, if I don't wish to receive any more books, I can return the shipping statement marked "cancel." If I don't cancel, I will receive 4 brand-new larger-print novels every month and be billed just $5.24 per book in the U.S. or $5.99 per book in Canada. That's a savings of at least 19% off the cover price. It's quite a bargain! Shipping and handling is just 50¢ per book in the U.S. and 75¢ per book in Canada.* I understand that accepting the 2 free books and gifts places me under no obligation to buy anything. I can always return a shipment and cancel at any time. Even if I never buy another book, the two free books and gifts are mine to keep forever.

161/361 IDN GHX2

Name   (PLEASE PRINT)

Address   Apt. #

City   State/Prov.   Zip/Postal Code

Signature (if under 18, a parent or guardian must sign)

Mail to the **Reader Service:**
IN U.S.A.: P.O. Box 1867, Buffalo, NY 14240-1867
IN CANADA: P.O. Box 609, Fort Erie, Ontario L2A 5X3

* Terms and prices subject to change without notice. Prices do not include applicable taxes. Sales tax applicable in N.Y. Canadian residents will be charged applicable taxes. Offer not valid in Quebec. This offer is limited to one order per household. Not valid for current subscribers to Harlequin Heartwarming larger-print books. All orders subject to credit approval. Credit or debit balances in a customer's account(s) may be offset by any other outstanding balance owed by or to the customer. Please allow 4 to 6 weeks for delivery. Offer available while quantities last.

Your Privacy—The Reader Service is committed to protecting your privacy. Our Privacy Policy is available online at www.ReaderService.com or upon request from the Reader Service.

We make a portion of our mailing list available to reputable third parties that offer products we believe may interest you. If you prefer that we not exchange your name with third parties, or if you wish to clarify or modify your communication preferences, please visit us at www.ReaderService.com/consumerschoice or write to us at Reader Service Preference Service, P.O. Box 9062, Buffalo, NY 14240-9062. Include your complete name and address.

HW15

YES! Please send me **The Montana Mavericks Collection** in Larger Print. This collection begins with 3 FREE books and 2 FREE gifts (gifts valued at approx. $20.00 retail) in the first shipment, along with the other first 4 books from the collection! If I do not cancel, I will receive 8 monthly shipments until I have the entire 51-book Montana Mavericks collection. I will receive 2 or 3 FREE books in each shipment and I will pay just $4.99 US/ $5.89 CDN for each of the other four books in each shipment, plus $2.99 for shipping and handling per shipment.*If I decide to keep the entire collection, I'll have paid for only 32 books, because 19 books are FREE! I understand that accepting the 3 free books and gifts places me under no obligation to buy anything. I can always return a shipment and cancel at any time. My free books and gifts are mine to keep no matter what I decide.

263 HCN 2404   463 HCN 2404

Name _____ (PLEASE PRINT)

Address _____ Apt. #_____

City _____ State/Prov. _____ Zip/Postal Code _____

Signature (if under 18, a parent or guardian must sign)

Mail to the **Reader Service:**

IN U.S.A.: P.O. Box 1867, Buffalo, NY 14240-1867
IN CANADA: P.O. Box 609, Fort Erie, Ontario L2A 5X3

READERSERVICE.COM

Manage your account online!

- Review your order history
- Manage your payments
- Update your address

*We've designed the
Reader Service website
just for you.*

Enjoy all the features!

- Discover new series available to you, and read excerpts from any series.
- Respond to mailings and special monthly offers.
- Connect with favorite authors at the blog.
- Browse the Bonus Bucks catalog and online-only exculsives.
- Share your feedback.

Visit us at:

ReaderService.com